RULE #1: YOU CAN'T DATE THE COACH'S DAUGHTER

THE RULES OF LOVE SERIES

ANNE-MARIE MEYER

To Logan and Emily
My adorable cover models.
You were a BLAST to work with.

CHAPTER ONE

THE CALIFORNIA HEAT beat down on me as I stood next to the table. Five minutes left and then football practice was done for the day. That meant I only had five minutes to stand there and pretend that I wasn't staring at Tyson Blake.

But how could I not? He was the epitome of perfection in his six-foot-two, incredibly toned, smells-good-even-when-he-sweats, senior body. And he was off limits. If dad even got a hint that I liked Tyson, I'd be sent off to Catholic school, where I'd be forced to become a nun.

Nope. I had to be discreet. Which I had gotten pretty good at. I'd spent years convincing Dad that boys were the last thing on my mind.

Ha.

"Hey, Tiny."

I jumped at the sound of Dad's voice. Tiny. The lovely nickname given to me by my father that has carried over to the entire football team. Nothing like being reminded everyday just how short you really are.

I whipped my gaze over to find Dad staring at me. I'd been filling the last-minute water cups. Nerves raced through my stomach. Had he been reading my mind? Did he know that I was thinking about Tyson?

I shrugged, trying to look inconspicuous. "What?" I called out.

"You're watering the grass."

I glanced down at the cup I had been filling. Apparently, I was terrible at multi-tasking. I'd been too fixated on Tyson as he jogged across the field with his helmet off and his damp hair clinging to his forehead. The water had sloshed over the side and all over my Converses.

"Sorry," I yelled back, raising the cup to show that everything was good. I set it down on the table and sighed. What was the matter with me? First day of school and I was already slipping up. Thankfully, I'd convinced my dad that I didn't have to go to all the summer football camps with him, trading in my water-girl apron for one at In–N-Out.

It was really an act of self-preservation. Dad needed to think that I didn't like boys. And going to a camp where they only wore football pants and strutted around with their shirts off? Nope. I only had so much self-control.

Keeping him believing that I wasn't interested was really the only option. It kept his overprotective tendencies from spiraling out of control.

I set the last cup down on the table and straightened.

Heat crept up my neck, so I reached up and pulled my long and—most of the time—frizzy brown hair into a bun.

"That's brutal, Tiny. Having your dad around all the time," a deep, joking voice said from behind me.

I squeaked and turned. I knew that voice. Tyson Blake was standing inches away from me. My gaze met his brilliant blue eyes, turning me speechless. Now I knew what it was like to be a deer in headlights. My brain screeched to a halt.

"I—um—da—" I slammed my mouth shut before I let more nonsensical sounds escape my lips.

Tyson raised his eyebrows as he leaned toward me. My heart hammered in my chest. What was happening? Was he going to kiss me like I'd played out so many times in my head? Was he going to hug me? Do I hug him back?

Before I could stop myself, I raised my arms. There was no way I wasn't going to give Mr. Popularity a hug when offered one. Just as I began to close my arms around him, he stopped and straightened.

A water cup came into view. Heat raced across my skin, and I pulled my elbows in tight, praying that he hadn't seen my humiliating blunder. Thankfully, all he did was glance down at me as he drained the cup, crumpled it, and threw it —*swish*—into the trashcan behind me.

"Thanks, water girl," he said as he gave me a wink and turned away.

That's when I realized that my dad, the head coach, was standing behind him with a very unpleasant expression.

"Boss," Tyson said, nodding toward my dad.

My mind swirled. Even though Tyson hadn't seen my aborted hug, my dad had. And he was not happy about it.

"Mr. Blake, what's taking so long?" he asked, straightening. Even at his tallest, he was dwarfed by Tyson.

Tyson smiled at him and then flicked his gaze over at me. I shot him an I-don't-know-why-my-dad-is-acting-crazy look.

"I was just getting some water," he scoffed as he motioned toward the table.

My dad did not look convinced. He snapped his gaze over to me. "This true?" he asked me.

"Why would I lie about that?" Tyson stepped forward.

"It's true," I blurted out, praying that my dad wouldn't ask me why I'd just tried to hug the star quarterback.

He must have sensed my plea, since he turned his attention back to Tyson. He held up a finger. "What is the number one rule?"

Tyson glanced over at me and then back to my dad. "Never hit on or try to date the coach's daughter," he said, holding up his hands.

Dad stepped forward. "And don't forget that."

Tyson laughed. "Trust me, I wouldn't dream of it." Then he took off, jogging over to where his minions stood, waiting for him so they could head back to the school.

Once Tyson was gone, I turned to my dad, who gave me a satisfied nod and then made his way over to Xavier, the assistant coach. Dad picked up his clipboard, and they bent their heads together.

I glared at him. I couldn't believe that he'd completely embarrassed me in front of Tyson like that. I was never going to forgive him.

"Thanks a lot," I muttered as I started handing out cups to the football players who had jogged over. Tyson was never going to be able to look at me without seeing my huffing, angry father. I was a social pariah. I might as well call in sick for the rest of the year.

Once the entire team was hydrated, I lifted the jug and set it on the grass. Then I turned back to the table and started folding it up.

"How'd practice go?"

I glanced over to see Rebecca, my best friend, walking up to me. Her cheeks were pink, and she was sweating. She was cheer co-captain and my best friend since we were in diapers. How she stayed with me through my frizzy, short hair and braces boggled my mind. We were literally Beauty and the Beast.

I groaned in frustration as I slammed down hard on the brace of the table leg and it folded in. "Terrible. I almost hugged Tyson, and my dad was here to make sure he knew that I was off limits."

I slammed the other leg down and yelped as I caught my thumb in the folding bracket. I lifted my hand to my mouth, wincing as the pain shot through my thumb.

"Oh, no. Man, your dad isn't going to let off this year,

huh?" Rebecca asked. She finished folding the table for me and turned it on its side so she could grab the handle.

I grabbed the bag of cups and the now-empty jug and followed after her. "Nope, doesn't look like it. First day back with the team, and he's already on high alert. I don't get it. It's like he blames me for my mom leaving. He's convinced that a boy is going to woo me and lead me down the path of, I don't know, whoredom?"

Mom dropped a bomb three years ago when she announced that she was leaving my dad to live in Cancún with her massage therapist, Pedro. Ever since then, when it came to me and guys, Dad was less than thrilled. He—on many occasions—has declared that he would rather experience a root canal with no anesthesia than see me date a high school boy. Or any boy. Ever.

And since he was the gym teacher and head football coach, he made it his life's mission to make sure that romance and I never collided.

"It's not that bad, Destiny. At least your dad cares enough to watch out for you. My dad? He couldn't be bothered to pick up the phone to wish me a happy birthday. Instead, he calls to tell me the twins are now a yellow belt in karate, which means they can poop rainbows or something." She rolled her eyes.

"I'm sorry, Bec." I sighed, blowing a loose strand of hair from my face. "Dads suck sometimes."

She nodded. Then an excited smile spread across her lips. "You'll never believe who I have in my pre-calc class."

She wiggled her eyebrows. A look only reserved for Sam Wilson.

"Really? That's lucky," I said, shifting the bag and jug to one arm so I could pull open the door that led to the gymnasium.

"I'd say. And, I get to sit next to him because Mr. Dawson is all, 'everyone sit according to the alphabet.' Wilson. Williams." She shrugged her shoulders. "Bless that strange, OCD man."

I smiled at her as we walked to the door in the far wall. Just on the other side was my dad's office. And just beyond that. The boy's locker room.

Where Tyson was.

Showering.

I cleared my throat as I forced all the thoughts that would have my dad boiling mad at me from my head. "Well, I hope you guys finally talk." I gave her a serious expression. "It's time."

Rebecca walked through the door that I held open. Once we were in the small hallway, I stopped in front of my dad's office, grabbed the key from my pocket, and unlocked the door.

"Baby steps, little one," she said leaning the table against a wall in the office.

"Well, don't wait too long. He's headed for college next year." I set the bag of cups on the shelf and the water jug underneath it. I never understood why she was so nervous around guys. She was tall and blonde. And she's had curves since middle school. When she walked down the hall, boys had to pick their jaws up off the floor. I was sure she could walk up to Sam, demand that he let her wax his legs, and he would lay down in submission. "Besides, he'd be an idiot not to date you."

Her cheeks hinted pink as she studied her nails. If I didn't love her as much as I did, I'd hate her. She was like a Disney princess. When she sang, wildlife collected around her feet.

"I just want it to be right," she said.

"Okay," I said nodding to her. Truth was. I had no idea. She had more experience in the guy department. She'd even kissed a guy before. Me? Nothing. Nada. Zilch.

Well, unless you count Porter Jones in the second grade. But that was more of a bite, on his part, than an actual kiss. I'm pretty sure that kissing involves lips colliding, not teeth. Porter didn't seem to have gotten that memo.

She glanced down at her watch. "I gotta go. I have homework, and then my dad's picking me up because I have to see the twins do...something. I really don't know. I stop listening when he mentions those brats."

"Thanks for helping me, Bec."

She gave me a quick hug and sprinted from my dad's office.

Now alone, I glanced around. Dad was still a half hour from leaving, and even though I've had my license since last summer, he insisted on driving me home.

I sighed and made my way over to the wall of team

photos. There was one for every year that my dad had been coach of the football team, tacked up with tape.

Somehow—I don't know how—my gaze found Tyson in last year's photo. His hair was shorter then. And he looked skinnier. But he was as handsome as ever. I leaned in closer, studying his lips and his perfect nose.

"You okay?"

For the second time that day, Tyson's voice filled my ears. I yelped and turned to see him leaning against the doorway. He had his eyebrows raised and a hint of a smile on his lips. He was dressed in jeans and a t-shirt that hugged his chest. I could smell his soap. It had a woodsy hint to it.

"Yeah. Um-hum," I said. Finally, coherent words. Sort of.

"I was looking for the Boss, but I'm guessing he's not in yet." He scanned the office.

"You guessed right, sir," I said, saluting him. Then heat rushed across my skin. What was I saying? What was wrong with me? I pinched my lips together to cut off any other ridiculous reactions.

He studied me for a moment and then glanced down the hall. "Bummer." He sighed. "Can you let him know I need to talk to him?"

I nodded.

Tyson studied me for a second longer before he turned. He took a step forward and then held his hand up. "Could you just tell him that I talked to you with other people around? I don't want him knowing that we spoke alone in his office." He grimaced. "I really hate running laps."

My stomach sank. It was confirmed. No boy was ever going to talk to me. Ever.

My name, Destiny "Tiny" Davis, was synonymous with pain and vomit. Well done, Dad. Well done.

"Sure," I said. My voice came out in a whisper as a defeated feeling settled in my chest.

There went any chance I would ever have to show Tyson that I was a cool person—that he was crazy not to get to know me. All he saw when he looked at me was the large, neon red sign my dad had placed above my head that said DO NOT TOUCH. In large capital letters.

"Thanks." He smiled and the disappeared around the corner. And probably out of my life forever.

I sank down onto one of the stained chairs in my dad's office and blew out my breath. This was going to be my life. My big, fat, sucky, junior year life. I might as well get used to it.

CHAPTER TWO

THE NEXT MORNING, I sat in first period, tapping my pencil on my chemistry book. I was waiting for Mr. Barnes, the seventy-five-year-old chemistry teacher, to walk through the doors and get started.

People were milling around, either standing by their tables or sitting in a cluster of lab stools. Everyone had someone to talk to. Except me.

It was probably my fault. That's what happens when you take an advanced class. Most everyone here was a senior. But I was okay with that. It was better than being stuck in Gen Chem.

Movement by the door caught my gaze. I glanced over to see Tyson walk in. Instantly butterflies erupted in my stomach. I focused on the crisp, clean notebook paper in front of me. How did this happen? I have a class with Tyson?

When I glanced up again, Tyson had moved from the

doorway over to Brutus, one of his posse members. They did a bro-shake and then Tyson sat down at the table with him.

Of course he would sit with his friend. Why was I so delusional as to think that he would sit next to me? I was a nobody.

Before I allowed myself to wallow in self-pity, a slender woman in sharp heels entered. The class grew silent as she scanned the room. She had a stack of books in the crook of her arm.

"Good morning," she said, walking over to Mr. Barnes's desk and placing her belongings on top of it. We were all watching what she was doing.

I could hear whispers in the back. Something about Mr. Barnes.

The woman shuffled a few things around and then straightened. "I am Ms. Swallow. I will be replacing Mr. Barnes."

"Did he die?" someone from the back asked.

She glanced in their direction. "No, Mr. Barnes did not die. But he is in the hospital. He had a nervous breakdown and went there last night."

The murmuring grew louder.

Ms. Swallow held up her hands. "I'm sure you are all worried for him. But I can assure you that he is in good hands and recovering quickly." She clasped her hands together and stepped out from behind the desk. "Because he will not be returning, I will be picking up where he left off.

Since this is only the second day of school, I'm anticipating that this will be an easy transition.

"Now, I've looked over Mr. Barnes's curriculum, and while it taught the basics, it did not go into the detail that I had hoped." She ran her gaze over the room. "So I have made changes. If you decided to take this class for an easy A, I will tell you that will not be the case. With the proper amount of work, you will leave my class with a deeper understanding of chemistry, which will carry you through college."

There was a collective groan. A few students stood and made their way to the door stating they needed to talk to Mr. Applegate, the school counselor.

I was cheering inside. Finally, a teacher who wasn't scared to challenge their students. I had to refrain from clapping.

When I saw Brutus sling his backpack over his shoulder, I half-expected Tyson to follow after him. But, he didn't. I snuck a peek back at him. He had an uneasy expression as he glanced down at the table in front of him.

Why wasn't he leaving? It wasn't a secret that his grades were subpar. Why was he sticking with a class where the teacher literally just told him that she was going to challenge him?

Before I could delve deeper into my curiosity, Ms. Swallow made her way to the front of the classroom and grabbed a stack of papers. She began handing them out and talking about her plans for the class.

"And now for partners." She tapped her chin as she glanced around. "Well, I guess the old alphabet trick has never let me down. Might as well continue it."

Once she located the class list, she began to read off names. As people were called, the sound of lab stools scraping against the floor filled the air.

"Blake..."

My ears perked at Tyson's name. Hope filled my chest for a moment before I reminded myself that there was an entire letter between his name and mine.

"Carter."

Of course. Brutus. How guys like Tyson were so lucky to magically get paired with their friends boggled my mind. But me? I'd probably be stuck with the kid who licks the beakers.

"Brutus Carter?" Ms. Swallow called out.

And then realization hit me. Brutus had left. Maybe—

"Alright, since there is no Mr. Carter, let's see...Davis."

And my stomach sank to the floor. I closed my eyes as I waited for her to admit that this was all a joke and that there was no way on God's green earth I was going to be paired with Tyson Blake.

But the scraping of chair legs surrounded me, and Ms. Swallow began calling more names.

"This seat taken?" Tyson asked.

I swallowed, counted down from three, and opened my eyes. "No," I squeaked. Great. Every time I talked to Tyson I sounded like an idiot.

He glanced over at me and then pulled his notebook from his backpack. "I hope the Boss will be okay with this." He held up his hands. "It's mandatory. He can't get mad at me if another teacher is forcing us to talk."

Ouch. *Forced* to talk.

I let out a nervous giggle and turned back to the list that Ms. Swallow had included in the packet she'd handed out. Truth was, I wasn't sure how my dad would feel about me getting paired with Tyson. I was about 99% sure he'd hate the idea. But like Tyson said, it was mandatory. Dad couldn't very well march up to Ms. Swallow and demand that we change lab partners. Could he?

The rest of class was spent going over the syllabus and Ms. Swallow's expectations. By the end, I was pumped to be taking this class. She had a lot planned, and it excited me.

Tyson, on the other hand, looked less than thrilled. He packed up his notebook, shouldered his bag, and headed out of the room.

I sat back in my chair, watching his retreat. A bubble of excitement exploded in my stomach. I was partnered with Tyson. Me. Girl that was banned from ever talking to a boy. Ever.

I grabbed my belongings, shot Ms. Swallow a smile, and headed out into the hall. I was supposed to meet Rebecca at my locker so we could walk to second period together.

Thankfully, she was waiting for me when I arrived. My smile must have tipped her off because she raised her eyebrows.

"What's with you? Why are you so happy?"

I shrugged as I pulled open my locker door and slipped the beast that was my calc book onto the top shelf. "You will never believe what just happened to me," I said, glancing over at her.

Her eyes widened. "What?"

Taking a moment to bask in what had just happened, I turned and took a deep breath. "Tyson is in my Chem class and is partnered with me."

"No!"

"Yes! Mr. Barnes had a panic attack, so he's gone. And the new teacher did the OCD method to pair us up, and D comes after B, so..." I turned back around to grab my art book and slammed my door.

Rebecca was nodding. "Nice. Now your dad can't say anything if he talks to you. It's teacher ordered. You have to get to know Tyson Blake." Rebecca wrapped her arms around her books as we headed down the hall. "It's perfect."

I spent the rest of the day too excited to focus. I wanted to get to practice to see if Tyson was going to treat me any different. Part of me hoped that he'd walk up to me and ask me something. And when my dad came over, we'd just wave him away, saying it had to do with school.

So, when the bell rang at two o'clock, I practically sprinted down to my dad's office. He was sitting at his desk doing paperwork.

"Hey, Tiny," he said when I walked in, dropped my backpack on the floor, and collapsed in my chair.

He seemed like he was in a good mood. I debated on whether I should tell him about my new lab partner or wait.

Knowing he would most likely ruin my excitement, I went with wait.

"Hey, Dad." I glanced around the room while he kept writing on a piece of paper. "Do you know about the new Chem teacher we have? Ms. Swallow?"

He glanced up at me with wide eyes. His expression threw me off as he mumbled something like, there were a lot of teachers and how was he supposed to know just one. Then he turned his attention back to his paperwork.

I studied him. That was weird. Was he not telling me something? Instead of asking, I just brushed it off. "I'm excited to be in her class. She's really nice, and she's going to be a good teacher. I can tell."

He nodded and then looked up. "Jug, hon," he said, pointing the tip of his pencil at the big and circular, orange water cooler I had put away yesterday.

Right. If he wasn't focused on killing my love life, Dad only thought about one thing. Football.

I grabbed the table, jug, and bag of cups and shuffled out of his office. It was a long walk out to the field by myself. Unfortunately for me, no one on the team would ever think of helping. They were too worried about the laps they would have to run if my dad caught them.

Just as I pushed open the gymnasium door to head outside, the table slipped from my grasp and crashed down on my foot.

I yelled and jumped, sending the jug tumbling down to the ground. The noise echoed off the gym's high ceilings and hardwood floors. I bent down to pick up what I'd dropped, grateful no one had been around to see me.

"You need help?" Tyson asked.

I glanced up to see him, dressed in his football uniform. The one that hugged him in all the right places. Bless the creators of football uniforms.

I swallowed. What was I supposed to say? I wanted to say yes, even though I knew what my dad would do to him if he found Tyson anywhere near me. I couldn't help it. When the captain of the football team and most likely to be home-coming king asks you if you want help, you say yes.

So I obeyed that one very obvious rule. "Yes," I said, nodding my head a bit too vigorously.

Calm down, Tiny. He's just helping you with the water set-up, not giving you a kidney.

So I slowed my nod and tried to act relaxed. "That would be okay, I guess."

He glanced over at me as he bent down and picked up the jug that had rolled across the gym floor. I bent down to pick up the table. When I straightened, I yelped.

Tyson had magically appeared right next to me.

"You're a ninja," I said, the words slipping out. I winced. Who says that?

"What?" he asked. When I glanced up at him, I saw that his lips had tipped up into a smile. "Did you just say ninja?"

I scoffed. How the heck was I going to get out of this?

Deciding it would be best to just roll with it, I shrugged. "You've never been told that?"

He shook his head. "Not even once."

I'd been so focused on watching his expression that I didn't notice he'd reached out to grab the table from me until his fingers brushed against my own. I swallowed as I glanced down. His fingers were touching mine. Mine!

I let go, snapping my hand back, and glanced around. I half expected my dad to come barreling into the gym, all red-faced and snarling. But nothing happened.

I let out the breath I had been holding. When I glanced over, Tyson was studying me. I felt like I needed to say something.

"Thanks for that," I said, nodding toward the table. I took a few steps back, just in case good ole Dad saw us.

He shot me a smile. "No problem. The table is about the same size as you."

"Hey," I said, shooting him a stern look. I turned and pushed open the door, holding it as he walked through. "Only a select few people can make fun of my height."

He shrugged as I let the door shut behind us. The heat clung to my skin. I led the way down to the field. Tyson had grown silent, and I wondered if I had offended him. As I replayed our conversation over in my mind, I couldn't figure out how that could have happened. He'd made fun of my height. Right?

"Can I ask you something?" His voice had grown so quiet, I wondered if I had heard him right.

Grateful I hadn't offended him, I glanced over. "Sure." Then I backpedaled. "Well, it depends on what you want to know." I pushed my hair from my face. It clung to my skin like octopus tentacles. I should have put it up in to a ponytail before coming outside.

"Are you smart? Like, really smart?" He glanced over at me, his eyes a deep blue.

"Um." How was I supposed to answer that. Was this a humility test? If I said yes, I'd sound conceited. If I said no, well, that would be a blatant lie. So I settled with, "Sort of?"

His eyebrows knit together. "How is someone *sort of* smart?"

We were at my usual spot, so I dropped the bag of cups onto the ground and waved for him to hand me the table. He shook his head, set the jug down, and began to unfold it. Not sure what to do, I stood back, watching his perfectly formed muscles move as he set it up.

"Well, I'm not sure how to answer that without sounding conceited." I pulled my hair back into a bun at the nape of my neck.

When he stood and glanced over at me, I could have sworn I saw his gaze hesitate on my neck. I blinked, and he was back to looking at my eyes. It was my imagination. It had to be.

"So you are smart. I figured that since you were in a senior Chem class." He sighed and ran his hand through his hair. "Do you tutor? Like, could you help me with Chem?"

My heart hammered so hard that I thought it might leap

from my chest and take off down the field. Was Tyson Blake asking me for help?

He widened his eyes. "Oh, it wouldn't be anything like that. It would just be one lab partner helping another lab partner out." He held up his hands, as if spending time with me outside of a school assignment would be absurd.

I tried to not let that hurt my feelings. He was probably just trying to protect himself. If my dad caught wind of any of this, the answer would be a flat-out no, and Tyson would be running laps from now until graduation.

"Of course," I scoffed. "I knew that." Other football players began to appear on the field. I knew my dad was moments behind them. My mind raced as I tried to come up with a way to pull this off.

"Here," Tyson said, reaching out and grabbing my hand. Tingles erupted from his touch and raced up my arm. "Do you have a pen?"

I shook my head.

"Hmm." He glanced around, while still holding my hand. I couldn't focus on anything other than how small my fingers looked next to his.

Suddenly, he dropped my hand and bent down, grabbing a stick. He wrote the number 714-555-9823 in the dirt. "That's my number," he said, motioning toward it. "Text me when you've decided."

"BLAKE!" my dad bellowed.

My stomach sank as I glanced up to see Dad barreling

toward us. His face was red, and his gaze was fixed on Tyson.

"I gotta go," he said, turning and running to meet my dad.

After a brief exchange, Tyson's shoulders dropped, and he began a slow jog around the field. My dad turned to stare at me. He pointed at me and then to the jug. I sighed as I nodded and picked up the bag of cups to set them onto the table.

And then my gaze made its way over to Tyson's number. To his personal cellphone—that he gave me permission to text. I blinked a few times, but the numbers remained, scratched into the dirt.

I was going to talk to Tyson Blake again.

CHAPTER THREE

PRACTICE SEEMED to drag on and on. By the time my dad blew the whistle and the players made their way off the field, I'd memorized Tyson's phone number—which I promptly erased. I'd also woven a bunch of blades of grass and successfully built a pyramid with the cups.

Tomorrow, I was going to bring my backpack and get a jump start on my homework.

After the football players were hydrated, I packed up and headed back toward the school. Rebecca didn't have practice today, so that left me to lug the items in alone. Once they were successfully put away, I grabbed a notebook and a pen. I wrote Tyson's number down, just in case I hit my head and developed amnesia, and stuffed it into my backpack.

Then I waited for Dad to come back from the field.

It took about ten minutes for him to appear. He was talking to Xavier. Just as he entered his office, the now-clean football players began to emerge from the locker room. I tried hard not to stare, but I wanted to see Tyson again. I wanted to make sure that I hadn't dreamed up this whole situation.

Just as Tyson passed by the office door, my dad called out his name.

My stomach sank. Did he know that Tyson wanted to spend time with me? I glanced over at my dad and I relaxed a bit. He was flipping through his clipboard at his desk. His shoulders were relaxed, and his skin tone was normal.

"You called me, Boss?" Tyson asked as he stepped into the room.

My dad nodded. "You've been late the last few practices." He let the paper drop as he glanced up. "Is this something I should be worried about?"

I felt Tyson's gaze on me, but when I moved to meet it, he'd turned back to study my dad. I let my gaze linger on his face. How could anyone have such perfect features?

"I stopped by yesterday to apologize. I know the rule, and I promise it won't happen again."

My dad leaned forward. "It better not."

Tyson ran his hands through his hair. "Yep."

Dad scoffed and folded his arms. "You're not the only one who can be quarterback. Don't let that idea get cemented in your brain. If you don't take this seriously, I'll find someone who will."

Tyson's gaze made its way over to me. I studied my hands in my lap. For some reason, I didn't want him to think I was eavesdropping on their personal conversation, even though it was pretty hard not to, with me sitting right there.

"I get it." Tyson shrugged as if this didn't bother him, when I could see that it did.

My dad clenched his jaw but nodded. "Good. You can go." He set the clipboard down and began rifling through some stacks of paper on his desk.

I glanced up to see Tyson nod. As he turned to leave, his gaze met mine. After making sure my dad wasn't watching, he motioned with his thumbs for me to text him. I pinched my lips as I glanced over at my dad, who hadn't bothered to look up.

I nodded at Tyson and he smiled. Then he slipped from my dad's office and out into the hall. I couldn't help but wonder what that had been about.

Before I could delve too far into dissecting his intentions, my dad grunted from his desk. I could tell that Tyson had bothered him. Dad was serious about winning state this year, which meant he wanted his players to be just as committed.

His captain suddenly wanting to ditch out on a practice couldn't sit well with him.

"Do you know why he's been late?" His gravely voice broke through my thoughts.

I glanced over at him and shook my head. Hopefully, it didn't look too spastic. "No. Why would I know?" An uncomfortable feeling bubbled up in my chest, causing me to giggle a bit too high.

Dad studied me. "You two were talking on the field earlier. What was that about?"

I shrugged, hoping it came across as nonchalant. "I don't know what you're talking about. He just helped me bring the table out to the field. That was all." My eyes widened. Hopefully that hadn't been a mistake to confess.

A disgruntled look passed over his face, but he didn't freak out, which was nice. "Hmm." He tapped his pen on his desk and then leaned back in his chair.

"I'm sure it's nothing," I said, hoping to help him calm down.

He glanced over at me and sighed. "Yeah. You're probably right." He dropped his pen into the cup on his desk and smiled at me. "Ready to go? I was thinking we could grab a pizza on our way home," he said as he pushed his chair back and stood.

"Pizza, Dad? Really?"

"It's either that or my cooking."

I puffed out my cheeks like I was holding in vomit. "Ugh, pizza it is," I said, slinging my backpack onto one shoulder and following him out of his office.

"That's what I thought."

I SAT cross-legged on my bedroom floor later that night, staring at my phone that was sitting next to the paper with Tyson's number. I'd been trying to work up the courage to text him for ten minutes now.

He needed to know my answer. I'd decided that I wasn't going to break my dad's rule and hang out with a boy. After all, it wouldn't end well for Tyson. I would hate to find out what would happen to a guy who was caught alone with me.

"Just pick it up and text him," I whispered. My hand hovered over the phone. I could do this. It was just a text after all. An impersonal, easy form of communication.

As I lowered my hand to pick my phone up, it rang. I almost jumped out of my skin. Glancing down, I saw it was Rebecca. Good. A distraction.

"Hello?"

"Hey, Destiny. Whatcha doing?"

I sighed, flopping onto my back and staring up at the ceiling. "Ruining my own life."

Rebecca laughed.

"Hold on, I would actually have to have a life to do something like that." I sighed, blowing a strand of hair from my face. "Which I do not."

"What? Why are you being dramatic?"

I could hear the tapping of computer keys in the background. "Are you doing homework?" I asked.

The noise stopped. "I can talk to you and write a paper at the same time."

I groaned. What was happening to me? I'd been home for three hours now and I hadn't even cracked open my backpack. I should text Tyson and tell him that he was a fool to try to get involved with me. I wasn't smart, and the longer I put off my homework, the dumber I would become.

"I'm coming over," Rebecca said.

Before I could protest, she'd hung up the phone. I lay on the floor with my arm covering my eyes until there was a soft knock on the door.

"Tiny?" my dad called out.

"Yep," I said, not moving.

"Rebecca's here."

"I know."

The door opened, and I heard footsteps cross my hardwood floor. My bed squeaked, signaling that Rebecca had sat down on it.

"Why are you lying on your floor?"

I pulled my arm from my face and sat up. "You aren't going to believe what happened to me today."

I told her all about Tyson becoming my Chem lab partner. How he talked to me and how he gave me his number. Once I was finished, I lay back down on the floor. Even saying the words out loud didn't sound real. I stared at a stain on my ceiling while I waited for Rebecca to say something.

"So?" she finally asked.

I glanced over at her. "So what?"

She gave me an incredulous look. "What are you going to do?"

"What do you mean, what am I going to do? Bec, this is a boy we are talking about. The one creature on the planet my father has forbidden me from talking to. Alligators are just fine, but members of the opposite sex? He'd send me to a nunnery so fast." I covered my face with my hand.

Rebecca scoffed. "Listen, you might be making a bigger deal about this than you need to. Come on, he's a study buddy. Mandatory. If your dad has a problem with it, tell him to take it up with your teacher."

I dropped my hand. I could blame it all on Ms. Swallow. Sitting up, I wrapped my arms around my legs and pulled them to my chest. Was I making too big of a deal about this? Probably.

Just as my mind began to swirl with thoughts of Tyson and I hiding in the shadows of the library and studying chemistry, my stomach sank. There was no way I could pull this off. My dad would find out. It was better to stay away than try to make it work. I was too transparent. And besides, I couldn't lie to my dad. My mom had already hurt him enough with her deceit.

I sighed and picked up my phone. I punched in his number and then glanced over at Rebecca, who was shaking her head.

"I know that look. You're going to run away—tell him that you can't work with him." She grabbed a pillow and hugged it. "Come on, Des. You don't have to do this. You can be friends with a guy."

I shook my head. "It would kill my dad. I can't."

I typed my answer.

Me: Tyson, Tiny. I can't be your study buddy. Sorry.

I set my phone on the ground. A feeling of sadness washed over me. Which made me feel stupid. Why was I sad? From one conversation? Man, did I romanticize things. Perhaps it would be better for Tyson to stay away from me.

A second later, my phone chimed. Startled, I glanced down at it. Tyson had written me back. I picked up my phone and swiped it on. Why had he responded so fast?

Tyson: I'm calling you

Just as I read the words, his number flashed across the screen, and my phone's obnoxious ringtone filled the air.

"Who's calling?" Rebecca asked. She'd lain back on my bed with her knees up. Her music was on, and her foot was twitching to the beat.

"Tyson," I whispered. What was I supposed to do? Answer it?

Rebecca shot up. "What?"

I held up my phone. "Tyson. Tyson is calling me."

Her eyebrows rose. "Answer it!"

I scrambled to bring my phone back. "Right. Answer it. Okay." I hit the green button and brought it to my cheek. I took a deep breath. "Hello?"

"Destiny?"

He knew my real name?

"Yeah?"

"Hey. Tyson."

"I know," I blurted out.

"Oh. I got your message."

I pinched my lips and nodded. "Um-hum."

"Is there anything I can say to convince you to change your mind?"

I stared at Rebecca, who was watching me. I mouthed, "Oh my goodness." Her eyes were as wide as saucers.

"What's he saying?" she asked.

I waved her away. I couldn't be distracted right now. "Tyson, I'm just not sure this is a good idea. You know my dad. It's like the Taliban over here."

He chuckled. It was soft and melodious. "Right." He cleared his throat. "What if I promised you that we wouldn't get caught?"

I leaned back on my extended arm. "How would you ever keep that promise? My dad is everywhere."

"True." He sighed. "Listen, Tiny. I need your help. I..." His voice had become so low that I could barely hear him. He cleared his throat. "I just really need this. So what do you say? Help a guy out?" He sounded so hopeful that I was finding it very hard to say no.

"Listen, Tyson. I—"

"Hey," Rebecca said, waving her arms.

I glanced over. "What?"

"You can say we're studying. I'll lie for you."

Great. Now my best friend was an accomplice. "Bec, no."

"You still there?" Tyson asked.

I turned my attention back to the phone. "Yep. Sorry, my...cat's distracting me."

Rebecca raised her eyebrows.

"Cat?" Tyson asked.

"Yeah. He's making unnecessary sacrifices for me." I shot her a purposeful look, and she rolled her eyes.

"Sounds like a good cat." He let out his breath. "How about we try out tutoring for a week. If you decide that it's too much work, we can call it off. No hard feelings."

I hesitated. What he was proposing didn't sound terrible. Besides, we'd be studying, not proclaiming our love for each other. And Rebecca had already agreed to be my alibi. If we couldn't figure something else out, I could just lie, and tell my dad I was at her house.

Pushing away my fear, I nodded. "Sure. I can try."

"Really?" I could hear the enthusiasm in his voice.

"Really."

"Great," he said.

I moved to hang up, but I heard him call out my name. I brought the receiver to my ear. "Yeah?"

"Thanks."

"No problem. Now, I need to go study, or I will have nothing to teach you."

He laughed. "Sounds good. I'll see you in class tomorrow."

"Bye."

After we hung up, I flopped back down on the carpet and lay there. What had I done? Was I seriously going to hang out with Tyson? A giggle erupted in my throat. A nervous tick I've had since I was a kid.

"What's going on?" Rebecca asked.

I glanced over at her. "I'm so screwed."

CHAPTER FOUR

THE NEXT MORNING, my alarm sounded too soon. I'd been up half the night studying for chemistry the next day. I finally crawled under my covers at two, only to be woken at six. I yawned and stretched out on my bed.

An excited feeling started in my stomach and exploded throughout my body.

I had a *date* with Tyson Blake.

Well, study date. But at this moment, I was going to revel in the thought that I had a planned event with Tyson. No matter the reason.

When my alarm sounded again, I turned it off and rolled out of bed. Once I was showered, I stood in front of my closet, trying to figure out what I was going to wear. A dress? Shorts? A skirt?

I groaned as I threw my last pick, a plaid, pleated skirt, onto my bed. Why was I stressing about this so much? In the past, I would have just thrown on my signature t-shirt and jeans. Would Tyson even care what I was wearing?

For some reason, our first time hanging out felt as if it should be special. I didn't want to mess this up.

Twenty minutes later, I settled on a blue floral dress that I got last year for my Aunt Vivian's wedding. After I slipped on a pair of strappy sandals, I grabbed my backpack and phone and headed downstairs.

Dad was up and making a huge plate of eggs. His eyes widened when he saw me.

Crap. My clothes were going to tip him off. Why had I decided to get dressed up? If he found out what was going on, this not-a-date would be over before it had even begun.

"Wow, Tiny. You look amazing," he said as he dumped a spoonful of eggs onto a plate and handed it to me. Just as I reached out to take it, he tightened his grip. "Why do you look so nice? Are you trying to impress someone?"

I let out an exasperated groan. "Seriously, dad? No. What boy would ever want to date me?" This conversation with him was making me about as comfortable as when I was twelve and my dad sat me down to have the "so your body is changing" talk.

He narrowed his eyes. "You know why I don't want you to date," he said.

I sighed. "Yes. You don't want me to lose focus on what's really important." He loosened his grasp on the plate and let me take it. "Trust me dad, that's not going to happen."

He nodded as he grabbed his plate and followed me to

the table. "You say that, honey, but I've seen it so many times. Girls going all gaga for a boy and BAM"—he slammed his hand down onto the table—"they end up pregnant and dropping out of school to run after their out-of-a-job boyfriend." He stabbed his eggs with his fork.

Great. All my dad saw me as was a hormonal teenager who only followed her biological urges. Instead of attempting to tell him that I was different—that I was actually responsible—I nodded and focused on my eggs. Just as I shoveled the last bit into my mouth, my phone chimed. I reached over and studied it.

My heart began to race when I saw the nickname I'd given Tyson. Chicken.

I blinked. Was he texting me? Again?

My phone chimed. Another one came in.

Dad glanced over at me, and then pointed to my phone with his fork. "You going to check that?"

I nodded and grabbed it, slipping it onto my lap.

"What's Rebecca want so early in the morning?" he asked. 'Cause only my best friend could possibly be texting me.

I swallowed. I hated lying to my dad. But confessing that it was one of his players was not an option for me. "She's just clarifying some things we needed for Pep Group tonight."

Pep Group. The only after school activity my dad let me participate in. Probably because it was sparsely attended. No threat of boys with saggy jeans and side swept hair riding in on a motorcycle to take the virtue of his little girl.

No. It was just Rebecca, Samson, Jessica, and I. And most times, it was just me. Alone.

Dad smiled. "Well, you should answer then. We need lots of visibility for the football team this year. We're going to state," he said, nodding toward my phone.

I smiled and stood, taking my plate over to the sink. "Will do, Dad." I slipped into the living room so I could check my phone in peace. I didn't need Dad over my shoulder reading whatever Tyson had written.

Once I was in the clear, I glanced down at my screen. My heart hammered in my chest as I read his text.

Tyson: Tiny. Can we meet after practice today? Tried the homework but I suck.

A smile played on my lips. I'm sure he was overexaggerating his lack of ability. How could someone with so much perfection be bad at anything.

I clicked on the second text.

Tyson: Promise you won't think bad of me when you see how terrible I am?

I studied his words. Part of me wondered if he was flirting with me. Was that possible? I shook my head. I was being ridiculous. There was no way Tyson was flirting with me. I'm not in his social class. He's the star quarterback and most likely to become homecoming king. Running with the likes of me would just hurt his social status.

He was being nice. Plain and simple. And I was only going to do stupid things if I allowed myself to think anything different.

Me: Sure. Where do you want to meet?

I studied my phone, waiting for him to answer. After five minutes with no response, I slid my phone into my dress's pocket and headed back into the kitchen. I couldn't spend my whole morning waiting for him to respond. I'd drive myself crazy.

Dad was standing at the sink, rinsing the breakfast dishes. I walked over and pulled open the dishwasher. After everything was loaded, he turned.

"Ready to head to school?"

I nodded and grabbed my backpack.

Fifteen minutes later, I was in front of my locker, trying to ignore the fact that I still hadn't heard from Tyson. Why wasn't he answering? Last night, he'd been so quick to respond. I tried to tell myself it was probably because he was busy getting to school and not because he suddenly got scared and wrote me off.

I slammed my locker door and turned, making my way to Chem. I'd be seeing him in a few minutes, so I tried to calm my nerves. This is why I should never allow myself to like a guy. I end up becoming a walking idiot.

Once I was in the room and sitting at a lab table, I got out my notebook and chemistry book and stared at the last question I hadn't had time to finish last night.

The sound of a textbook landing on the table made me jump. I whipped my gaze up to see Tyson standing next to me. His normally cheery disposition had been replaced with frustration. I parted my lips to ask him what was wrong, but as soon as Tammy, a cheerleader, came over, his frown morphed into a smile.

They chatted for a minute, and I tried not to eavesdrop on their conversation. But it was hard when Tammy squealed and smacked Tyson's shoulder every chance she got. Apparently, Drew was throwing a party on Friday and Tyson just *had* to go to it.

Of course she didn't invite me, even though I was sitting inches away from Tyson. I might as well have been a fly on the wall with how much attention she gave me. I tried to brush it off. It wasn't like my dad would let me go anyway.

Tyson smiled at her and said he'd try but he couldn't promise anything. I tried not to notice the change in the tone of his voice. Instead of accommodating and carefree, it was strained. Like he was hiding something. I wondered if it had anything to do with him being late to practice.

Ms. Swallow walked in, cutting their conversation short. I continued doodling on my notebook as they said goodbye and Tammy made her way over to her lab table. I became very aware of how alone Tyson and I were. I wanted to look over to see what he was doing, but I feared what I might say, so I kept myself preoccupied with the squiggly line I was drawing.

"You're quite the artist," he said.

My heart galloped as I glanced over at him. Tyson had a playful smile on his lips as he nodded toward my notebook. He was stupidly handsome. And he was talking to me.

"You're too kind," I said as I tucked my hair behind my

ear. "They're actually requesting I do a whole collection to showcase at the Louvre."

He raised his eyebrows. "France. Really." He nodded. "Well, that is something."

I laughed. "You didn't know you were paired with someone in such high demand."

He shook his head as he took out his notebook and pencil. "I didn't. But if that's the case, I'm glad we're partners."

I peeked at him from the corner of my eye as he flipped open his notebook. I saw him rub the back of his neck as he hunched over his homework. I'd never seen him look so out of place. When he walked into a room, he owned it. Every guy wanted to be him and every girl wanted to date him. All of that just to be taken down by chemistry.

"So, the homework didn't go well for you?" I asked, glancing over at him.

His gaze met mine, and my breath caught in my throat. His normally bright blue eyes had turned stormy grey and unsure. He shook his head. "No. I tried to figure it out, but I ended up confusing myself. That's why I need you, Tiny. You gotta help me."

His words washed over me. *I need you, Tiny.* It was like he had the ability to jump into my head and read my innermost thoughts. He knew exactly what I needed to hear. I swallowed as I turned my attention back to my book. I couldn't get wrapped up in every one of his words. They didn't mean what I so desperately wanted them to mean.

"I'm sure once I explain it, you'll be just fine." I shot him an encouraging smile.

Tyson studied me for a moment before he sighed. "Well, I'm excited to learn. Did you not get my text this morning?"

I tapped the end of my pencil on the table. "I answered back."

He drew his eyebrows together as he shifted to pull his phone from his pocket. Right as he clicked it on, the bell rang and Ms. Swallow clapped her hands.

"Mr. Blake, please put your phone away. Class has started."

Tyson parted his lips to protest, but Ms. Swallow shot him an uncompromising look. "Of course," he said, slipping it into his backpack.

Ms. Swallow spent the rest of class discussing the difference between a base and an acid. I kept thorough notes as she wrote on the board. When I glanced over at Tyson, he was doodling a picture in his notebook. Why wasn't he taking notes? If he was struggling this much in class, one would think he'd be trying his hardest to pay attention.

His phone buzzed, and he glanced around before he bent down to grab it. I tried hard not to notice, but I could see that it was a text from Tammy.

His shoulders shook as if he were laughing, then he turned in Tammy's direction. Acid rose up in my throat as I saw him nod toward her and type something on his phone.

I tried not to be frustrated. I tried to ignore the flirty texts they were sending back and forth between each other.

But, no matter how much I tried to justify what he was doing, anger built up inside of my chest.

Was this all an act? One of two things was going on here.

One, he didn't want to do the homework or learn about chemistry. But he knew that I was smart, and if he asked me, I'd fall over myself to help him out. After all, I was the sheltered dweeb who'd never been kissed.

Or two, it was some sort of sick bet. All the football players were trying to see what would actually happen to them if they were caught trying to date me. Was my dad crazy enough to enact some of the rumors that went around the school?

Either way, I didn't want to be a part of it. If Tyson was going to be like this, I was done. I may not have dated anyone, but I knew what I was worth. And I was worth a whole lot more than Tyson thought.

So I sat the rest of chemistry, rigid on my stool. I didn't glance over at him or try to analyze just how close he rested his elbow next to mine. I ignored his attempts at flirting when we started the acid/base lab Ms. Swallow gave us.

I wasn't going to be treated this way by any guy, much less Tyson Blake. He was going to have to find some other naive girl to fawn over him. Because I was out.

CHAPTER FIVE

THE BELL RANG. I gathered my things and hightailed it from the room before Tyson could talk to me. I ignored him when he called my name. Instead, I pushed through the door and out into the throng of people. I needed to get as far away from him as I possibly could.

I must have lost him in the crowd because he never caught up to me. I spent the rest of school trying to ignore just how painful it felt to watch him flirt with Tammy. I felt betrayed. I wasn't sure why, but the ache in my chest told me I'd been a fool.

There was no way Tyson had any feelings for me, and I was an idiot to have hoped he might.

When the final bell rang, I pulled out my phone to see I had a few missed messages.

One was from Rebecca, saying she was going to be a few minutes late to Pep Group. One was from my dad, reminding me that I was expected to go straight to Mr. Dominic's room for Pep Group. He even used the phrase, "no shenanigans."

And one was from Tyson.

I swallowed as my finger hovered over his message. I could read the first few words.

Tyson: Tiny. Got your text...

Did I want to open it? Did I want to read what he said? Had he noticed that I had pulled away—that I wasn't some doe-eyed girl anymore.

I took a deep breath and pressed on the trashcan instead. I didn't want to know what he said. I wanted to forget that I'd put my guard down for him. That I had lied to my dad for him.

It was better to be alone than hurt, that's what my dad had taught me. I hadn't realized until this moment how true those words were. Tyson had convinced me that I was special. That he wanted to be around me. It had all been a ruse. An easy way to get an A, and I fell for it.

Man, I was a fool.

I pulled open the door to Mr. Dominic's room and stepped inside. Samson and Jessica were sitting at one of the art tables, talking and laughing. I'd known them since kindergarten. They were nerdy, like me. And they both wanted to go to Harvard, so had joined as many after school activities as they could.

They couldn't hit the broad side of a barn, but they were enthusiastic and here. And I was seriously lacking for volunteers. With the first big game of the school year coming up, we needed all hands on deck.

I dropped my bag down on the table with a thud. Samson and Jessica turned toward me and smiled.

"Hey, Destiny. Have a good summer?" Samson asked. He pushed his glasses farther up his nose as he studied me. He had bright red hair that stuck up in odd directions, and his pale skin was covered with freckles.

I nodded. "Uneventful. Thankfully, my dad let me stay home instead of go to all those football camps."

Both Samson and Jessica nodded as if they understood my plight. They didn't. But it was nice of them to try.

Mr. Dominic walked in, halting our conversation. He nodded to us and then made his way to the back art closet and disappeared into it. I think Mr. Dominic was forced to be the advisor of the Pep Group. According to my dad, every teacher needed a group to lead and everyone figured that Mr. Dominic would be perfect for us.

Except, he wasn't thrilled to be stuck monitoring the four of us while we painted signs and planned activities that would help pump up the school for all the sports events. Most meetings, he just stayed in the art closet, planning lessons or rearranging paintbrushes.

"Bec coming?" Jessica asked, reaching up to tighten her ponytail.

I nodded and pulled out my notebook where I'd doodled some designs for the posters we could make. "Yeah. She had some cheer stuff to take care of, and then she'll be here." I was so thankful that my best friend had agreed to help me in Pep Group. She was beautiful and smart, and well above our social status. But she never made me feel like I was a burden, and wanted to help in anyway possible.

Plus, she could paint like a pro. It was her secret love. But her dad had informed her that she was headed to Harvard to get a law degree and eventually take over his firm. Lucky her.

They nodded and then stood and made their way over to the large paper rolls that lined the far wall. After ripping off a few pieces, we laid them out on a table, and I showed them my sketches.

About halfway through painting "One DREAM One TEAM" on the banner meant for the lunchroom, Rebecca rushed into the room. I smiled at her, using my wrist to push away the hair that had slipped from my bun.

"Glad you could join us," I said.

She smiled over at me, but it didn't have the normal breezy feel. She seemed stressed. I quirked an eyebrow, but she shrugged it off. I'd talk to her once we were done here. She probably didn't want to broadcast her issues in front of Samson and Jessica.

We spent the rest of the hour painting and listening to some Celtic music that Samson said we just had to hear. It was loud and upbeat. It wasn't my cup of tea, but it helped distract me from what had happened with Tyson earlier and right then, I needed that.

Once the paintbrushes were rinsed and drying, Samson

and Jessica left me and Rebecca to wait for the banner to dry enough for us to move it. I grabbed the bag of cookies I'd bought during lunch and motioned toward it. Rebecca nodded, and we ate half the bag before she sighed.

"What do you think of Colten?"

A cookie crumb flew to the back of my throat. I coughed and wheezed, pounding my chest. Rebecca raised her eyebrows, and I shook my head. After a few seconds, the tickle subsided, so I reached over, grabbed my water bottle, and took a sip.

"Colten? As in the school dropout?"

She wrapped her hair around her finger and got a far off look in her eye. I'd never seen her act this way about a guy. Ever.

"I would say I wouldn't be surprised if he ended up in juvie by the end of the year." Why was my friend acting all bashful about the school bad boy? Was she crazy?

She paused for a moment before she nodded and sat up even farther on her stool, propping her feet up on a nearby table. "You're right. I'm being stupid." She tucked her hands under her knees as she leaned forward.

I studied her, wanting to ask her to elaborate. But she didn't look like she wanted to, so I decided to drop it. I reached out and gingerly touched the globby paint on the "O". It was dry.

"Let's go hang this bad boy up, and then we can get out of here," I said, hopping off the barstool and waving over at her.

She smiled and followed suit.

We rolled it up, grabbed some of the heavy-duty tape, and made our way toward the walkway that ran across the top of the lunchroom. We stopped at the railing and lifted the banner over. I held onto one side as Rebecca unrolled it. I'd just placed the first bit of tape when someone cleared their throat behind me.

I ignored it as I ripped off another chunk of tape. It wasn't for me. Who would want to talk to me? Bec was already here, and she was the only one in this school who ever took the time to acknowledge me.

I moved to place the tape over the previous piece, but it folded in on itself. I groaned as I shook it, hoping it would magically unstick. More edges stuck together, and it was completely unusable.

"Here," Tyson said.

I jumped as I turned to see him standing behind me with a piece of tape. He had on a comical expression as he motioned toward the ruined piece in my hand.

My heart picked up speed, but I instantly shushed it. I couldn't be having these feelings for him. That was ridiculous. How could I have forgotten what had happened in Chemistry earlier?

But I needed the tape. I reached out, keeping one hand on the corner of the banner. "Thank you," I said, hoping I came across as relaxed and not like the nervous wreck I felt.

He extended it to me, and once my side was secured, I turned to him. Why did he have to look so good with his damp hair and incredibly tight jeans? Whoever had created them knew what they were doing. They looked like they were designed just for him.

And then I realized I was staring at his pants.

Heat raced to my cheeks as I turned and secured the banner with one more strip of tape. I made my way down the railing, taping as I went.

I wanted to talk to him, but I was worried that after a few words from Tyson, I'd forget my resolve and find myself doing his English homework as well. So I ignored him. What else was I supposed to do?

"Did you get my text?"

My skin burned. He was right next to me.

"No," I said. Truth was, I'd shut my phone off. I didn't want to obsess over every ring, wondering if it was a message from him.

"Huh, I swear I sent it." From the corner of my eye, I saw him reach down and pull his phone from his back pocket. He looked something over and then returned it. "Yeah, I sent it. That's weird that you didn't get it."

I cleared my throat. "I actually turned my phone off."

"Oh."

When I got to Rebecca's end, I found her leaning against the railing with an amused expression as she watched us.

"Hey, Tyson," she said, nodding toward him and then meeting my gaze and widening her eyes.

I pursed my lips, hoping she'd act cool. "Hey, Becca. Excited for the game on Friday?"

She nodded and waved toward the banner. "Can't you tell?"

Tyson leaned over the railing and then glanced at me. "Great sign."

A laugh escaped my lips. Was he serious? I doubted that in the two years I'd been president of the Pep Group, he'd even once looked at the signs we made. Why was he being nice to me? After his flirting escapade with Tammy, I was surprised he even remembered my name. And that thought hurt. A lot.

"Where's Tammy?" blurted from my lips.

Tyson's eyebrows rose as he studied me. "I'm not sure. Becca would probably know better." A confused expression passed over his face. "Are you guys friends?"

I snorted and grabbed the tape that Rebecca held in her hands and then turned to her. "I'm going back to Mr. Dominic's room. Thanks for helping." I passed by her and whispered, "I'll call you."

She nodded, said goodbye to Tyson, and made her way down the stairs.

I blew out my breath as I walked toward the art room. I was going to grab my backpack, walk home, and try to never think of Tyson Blake again.

But from the sound of Tyson's footsteps behind me, he wasn't going to leave me alone.

"Hey, are you okay?"

I felt his hand surround my elbow. He pulled on it, signaling me to stop. I hesitated but then complied. I didn't want to talk about it, but I also didn't like the way I was treating him. He didn't know that he'd done anything wrong. Who was I to tell him who he could talk to? We weren't even friends. I was the idiot who was making a big deal of it.

So I forced a smile and met his gaze. "Sorry. I'm just having a really bad day."

A look of concern passed over his face. I didn't know how to read it. Was it sincere? Or did he know what to do to calm down an emotional girl and get her to do what he wanted? I'd heard the stories. Girls were pretty much powerless when it came to Tyson. And from looking at the way his brow furrowed and his gaze softened, I was beginning to realize why.

"I'm sorry. I hope it wasn't because of anything I did."

I scoffed as I pushed open the art room door. The lights were out, which meant Mr. Dominic was gone. Relief flooded my chest. I was sure he wouldn't tattle on me to my dad, but I didn't want to risk it. It was better if only Rebecca knew that Tyson and I were talking.

I flipped on the light, walked over to the Pep Group's supply tote, and dropped the tape into it. I snapped on the lid and dragged it toward the edge of the table. I tensed as I pulled it, anticipating its weight, but then two arms wrapped around me.

"Let me," he said. His fingers brushed mine as he grabbed the handles.

My heart pounded so hard, I could hear it in my ears.

My mind felt so muddled that I couldn't really come up with a reason for him not to help. So I swallowed as I dipped down and stepped away from him.

He lifted the tote like it weighed next to nothing. I tried to ignore how his muscles flexed. I pulled my gaze upward when he glanced over at me. "Where do you want it?"

"Over there," I said, motioning toward the shelves along the back wall.

He nodded as he walked over and slid it into its spot. I hugged my chest. The memory of his arms wrapped around me felt burned on my skin. What was he doing here? Why was I letting my guard down?

Things never went well when Tyson Blake was involved. Hadn't I heard all the rumors that went around about him? He was a player. Dated girls and dumped them. Why was I so certain that he wasn't going to treat me the same?

Ugh. What was the matter with me? I wasn't dating Tyson. I was his tutor. His TUTOR. Why did I keep forgetting that?

He brushed his hands against each other and turned, shooting me one of his signature smiles. "So, now that's put away, is there anything else you need to do, or are you ready to get started?"

I swallowed as I studied him. I could do this. I could help him out. After all, I was a smart girl. I could keep my wits about me as I helped him pass Chemistry. So I forced a confident smile and nodded. "Sure. Where do you want to go?" I walked over and grabbed my backpack. "Your house?"

"No."

I turned. He'd said that fast and with more force than normal.

He looked sheepish as he shook his head. "I mean, no." Then he scrubbed his face with his hand. "And I'm guessing your place is off limits."

I laughed. Oh, he was funny. "Yeah, probably not a good idea. My dad would freak if I brought a boy home. And if that boy was you?" I sucked in some air. "If you have a death wish, then we can go there."

He laughed as he shouldered his backpack. "I kind of want to live, so..."

Hmm, a place to go. An idea floated into my mind. Hopefully, he wouldn't think I was dorky.

"Come on, I might know of a place," I said, throwing caution to the wind and waving at him to follow.

CHAPTER SIX

I SAT in Tyson's car, watching him round the hood and pull open the driver's door. Butterflies erupted in my stomach as I watched him get in and start the engine. It felt surreal. Was I really in his car, and were we really going some place together?

As he pulled out of his parking spot, the realization sank in. It was true. I was going to spend the afternoon with Tyson. My dad was going to kill me.

And just as I thought of him, my dad appeared a hundred feet off, on the sidewalk. I yelped and ducked down.

Tyson laughed and glanced at me. "You okay?"

I jerked my thumb toward the sidewalk. "My dad?"

His gaze made its way out my window, and his expression turned worried. "Yeah. Stay down," he said.

After a minute of driving, I peeked up at him again. "Is the coast clear?"

He nodded. "Yep. You can sit up."

I straightened, pushing some loose hair from my face. I glanced sheepishly over at him. "Sorry."

He shook his head. "Nope. You saved me from getting kicked off the team, so I should be thanking you." An uneasy expression settled on his features, and I wondered for a moment what that was about.

I thought about asking him, but then I realized that we didn't have that kind of relationship. So I just smiled, hoping he'd feel supported, and then turned my attention to my phone.

I still hadn't told my dad that I wouldn't be riding home with him today. Nerves built up in my stomach as I found his number and hit the message icon.

Me: Doing homework with Bec. Be home after dinner.

I hit send and then found Rebecca's number. I told her she was my alibi, and she responded with a smiley face.

Right after her message came in, my dad texted.

Dad: Sounds good. Have fun and I'll save you a plate of food in the microwave.

I blew out my breath as I tucked my phone into my backpack. Good, he bought it. I was in the clear. A weight felt as if it had been lifted from my chest. And then a little tug of guilt pulled at the back of my mind. I hated that I was lying to my dad. He was just trying to protect me, even if he was doing it in a ridiculous way.

"You okay?" Tyson asked. I felt his gaze on me, so I turned and smiled over at him.

"Yeah. Just letting my dad know I won't be home for dinner."

"Wow, we're going to study for that long?"

Embarrassment burned my skin. "I—um—" I had no idea what to say to that.

He laughed. "Relax, Tiny. Trust me, I need all the help I can get."

"Why?" Just as I asked the question, regret filled my chest. Why was I being nosy? He definitely didn't want to tell some junior his business.

Thankfully, he shrugged. "I figured that I'm graduating this year. Maybe it's time I started to give a crap." He twisted his hand on the steering wheel. "So, where are we headed?"

"Mason's Park."

He nodded as he flipped on his blinker and took a left. "Ooo, a park. Nice."

I tucked a loose curl behind my ear. "There's actually a tree house there."

"Tree house?" he asked. I watched as the corner of his lips tilted up.

Man, he had the best smile. It was confident and self-assured. Everything I was lacking. "Is that okay?"

He shrugged. "Sure. Who doesn't love a tree house?" he asked as he pulled into the parking lot of Mason's Park.

We gathered our things, and I led him through the woods to a small opening. It may have been illegal, but five summers back, Dad and I had spent the entire summer building this tree house. The city didn't seem to mind because they'd kept it up.

"Nice," he said.

I grabbed one of the slats we'd used to build a ladder up the trunk and pulled myself up. "It's pretty amazing."

Once we were both in the tree house, I realized this might not have been the smartest idea. Sure it was fun when I was a kid, but I'd grown since I last came here. And Tyson was even bigger. When we sat down, we took up the entire floor.

"It's cozy," Tyson said, stretching out his legs.

I could feel my cheeks burn. I wanted to say it was because of the heat that still clung to the evening air, but I was embarrassed. What kind of person has to hide their tutoring sessions?

Me. Only me.

"Yeah, I'm sorry. I'll come up with a better place next time."

Tyson laughed. It was soulful and free. It wasn't cocky, like he was trying to impress someone—it was genuine. And I liked it.

"No worries. I'll pick the place next time."

So there was going to be a next time. My heart rate

quickened at the thought. He wasn't scared of my dad or my complete lack of spatial reasoning.

"You want a next time?" I asked.

He glanced over at me, and I could see the humor in his expression. "Sure, Tiny. Why not?"

I pulled my notebook and textbook from my backpack. "Well, maybe we should get this session over with before you hire me as your full-on tutor. I may lead you down the wrong path."

He laughed harder this time, and I stared at him. What had I said?

"Oh, Tiny. I don't think you could lead me down the wrong path."

Realization hit me. "I didn't—I mean, that's not what I meant."

He reached out and patted my shoulder. "It's okay. I'll keep myself alert the whole time. Gotta stay away from the likes of you."

I studied him. Was it wrong that I felt a little offended that he thought I was this saint? I could break rules. I was doing that right now by being out with him.

"Hey, I'm pretty convincing," I said. "I've been known to corrupt people."

His laughter died down to a smirk. "Really. Who?"

I pursed my lips as I thought. There had to be someone I'd convinced to do something bad. "Ronnie. In the third grade. I convinced him to steal cookies from the lunch lady for me." I shot him a smug expression. "And he did."

He placed his hand on his heart, like a woman in one of those old Western movies. "Well, Destiny Davis, I didn't realize you were such a deviant. Whatever are we going to do with you?"

I laughed as I shook my head. Was it wrong that I was enjoying this so much? In the tree house, there was no dad or Tammy, it was just Tyson and I. It was nice.

"We should probably get busy if I am going to help you at all," I said, reaching over and grabbing my textbook.

Tyson grew quiet as he nodded and did the same.

The next hour flew by. It was nice to have chemistry to talk about. It was simple and straightforward. There were no hidden meanings or unspoken words. It was straight up numbers and facts. It was just what I needed to keep my mind from wandering into uncharted territory.

Our study session was interrupted when Tyson's phone went off. He shifted and pulled it out of his back pocket.

I tried not to stare at him as he studied his screen. Who had called him? Was it Tammy or another cheerleader? I made a mental note to ask Rebecca who he hung out with on the cheer team.

From the corner of my eye I saw his expression grow stony as he swiped his finger on the screen. Something wasn't right. After sending a quick response, he shoved his phone into his pocket and started to gather his things. I wanted to ask him what was wrong, but wasn't sure if it was my place.

I decided to ask anyway. "Everything okay?" I started

putting things into my backpack. Our study session must be over.

He paused and glanced over at me. My breath caught in my throat as I took in his gaze. He was upset. A desire to comfort him rushed through me. But I figured that physical contact would probably not be the best idea, so I gave him an encouraging smile and turned my attention to my backpack.

"Family issues," he said. His voice was low and full of frustration.

"I hear that," I said, the words tumbling from my mouth. *I hear that?* What was the matter with me? I cleared my throat and tried again. "Sorry. Anything I can do to help?"

He straightened and jumped from the tree house. I watched as he landed on his feet, as if jumping from seven feet up was an everyday occurrence.

I contemplated following suit but wasn't sure how I would explain a broken leg to my dad, so I took the ladder instead. Halfway down, I missed the rung and my foot slipped. I clung to the piece of wood in front of me, praying that I didn't look like a complete idiot.

Before I fell to my death, two hands wrapped around my waist. My heart pounded in my ears when I realized that Tyson was holding on to me.

"You okay?" he asked. His voice was inches from my ear. I could feel his warmth cascade over me.

"Yep. Mm hmm," I said. I reveled in the feeling of him so close to me.

He helped guide me the rest of the way down. Once I was on the ground, I pulled away, breaking our contact. Even though it was warm outside, my skin felt cool in the absence of his touch.

"Thanks," I said, tucking my hair behind my ear.

He shoved his hands into his front pockets. "Sure. Anytime." He shrugged, like rescuing a girl as she climbed down a ladder was nothing. And I wouldn't be surprised if it was.

We walked in silence to his car. Just as I climbed in and buckled my seatbelt, his phone went off again. He pulled it out. He cursed under his breath as he read the message. Sighing, he rolled his shoulders and glanced over at me.

"Do you mind if we make a pit stop before I bring you to Rebecca's house?" He glanced over at me, but I noticed a hint of hesitation in it. As if he were embarrassed by what he was asking me. What did Tyson Blake have to be embarrassed about?

I nodded. "Sure."

Ten minutes later, we pulled into the parking lot of Freddy's Tavern. I snuck a look over at him. His face was red, and his jaw clenched as he kept his gaze forward. I wanted to ask what we were doing here, but I didn't.

He hesitated, his fingers on the door handle. "I need to get my mom. Mind waiting here?"

"Of course." I wanted to tell him that I didn't judge him. That I knew what it was like to have less than perfect parents. But I doubted that he wanted to hear that right now. So I settled on an encouraging smile.

He studied me for a second before he nodded and pulled open the door. I watched as he disappeared into the tavern. I leaned against the seat and let out my breath as I stared at the building in front of me.

What was happening? It felt good that Tyson felt he could share this part of his life with me. From his playboy persona at school, I doubted that many people got to see this side of him. And yet, he was letting me in.

I was going to ignore the lingering thought that he *had* to bring me along. That I would have been stranded at Mason Park, where I would've had to call my dad and explain to him why I was there and not at Rebecca's.

Nope. I was definitely here because he felt safe around me.

The door of the tavern opened and Tyson appeared. He pushed open the door with his back and in his arms he carried a small woman. She had jet-black hair and was leaning her head against his shoulder. His jaw was clenched, but not from the weight of the woman. It looked as if he were carrying the weight of the world on his shoulders.

Without thinking, I opened my door and got out. I had an overwhelming desire to help.

"She okay?" I asked, taking note of her pale complexion.

Tyson nodded.

I pulled the back door open, and he set her inside. After he buckled her up, he slammed the door shut and scrubbed

RULE #1: YOU CAN'T DATE THE COACH'S DAUGHTER   63

his face. He tilted his gaze to the sky as he blew out his breath.

"I don't know why she keeps doing this," he said. His voice was low and coated in emotion.

Not knowing what to do, I stood there with my arms wrapped around my chest. I worried that if I didn't keep my hands occupied, I might try to reach out and hug him or something.

What was I supposed to say? Any answer to his frustration seemed ridiculous and forced. "I'm sorry," I whispered.

He dropped his gaze to meet mine. He studied me with an intensity that made me feel vulnerable—exposed. Then he nodded. "Let's get you back."

He walked to the driver's door and pulled it open.

I nodded, but doubted that he saw it. Once I was seated with my seatbelt on, he peeled out.

Tyson's mom was quiet the entire ride to Rebecca's. I glanced back at her to make sure she was still alive. She let out a few weak moans, and I saw her chest rise and fall—so I felt confident that she wasn't dead.

When Tyson pulled into Rebecca's driveway, he stared straight ahead with his hands clenching the steering wheel. I studied him, desperately wanting to say something to comfort him, to bring back that carefree laughter we shared in the tree house.

"Please, don't say anything," he said. His gaze dropped to his lap.

I reached out and rested my hand on his. Warmth raced

from my fingertips and exploded up my arm. But I kept my hand there. "I promise."

He met my gaze and held it. I wondered if he could read my mind. Did he see just what he was doing to me? Did I want him to know?

"Thanks, Tiny. I knew I could depend on you. You're the best kind of friend."

Friend.

I was Tyson's friend.

My heart pounded with relief. I'd graduated from crazy junior girl with an over-protective dad to someone he could talk to.

Unsure of what to do, I nodded, grabbed the strap of my backpack, and pushed open the door. After I shut the door behind me, Tyson raised a few fingers in a sort of half wave, half salute and then pulled out of the driveway.

I stood there alone. Trying to digest what had just happened. One thing was for sure, I wasn't ever going to be the same again.

CHAPTER SEVEN

REBECCA DROPPED me off at my house a half hour after Tyson left. I was grateful that she was quiet and didn't ask too many prying questions. It was hard enough trying to process the evening's events, and I really didn't need to speak about what had happened out loud.

She smiled over at me as I pulled open my door and hopped out. "I'm happy that it's working out for you. You know, with Tyson."

I shot her a look and peeked toward the house. Dad's light was on, which I hoped meant he was in his room instead of hiding behind the bushes to see if I were up to something.

"Yeah. Thanks for covering for me. I'm really happy to help Tyson out with his chemistry."

I wanted to tell her about what had happened. But I'd promised Tyson I wouldn't. Even though I trusted Rebecca with my secrets, for some reason it didn't feel right to trust her with his. What a strange place to be. Keeping secrets from my best friend for a guy.

Weird.

She nodded, and I started to shut the door. "Of course. You need to have some fun, Des. I'm happy to help."

I shot her a smile as she pulled out of my driveway.

Once I was in the house, I shut the front door as quietly as I could.

"Where have you been? It's late." Dad's voice was low. He was not happy.

I forced a smile and turned. "I was at Rebecca's."

He furrowed his brow as he studied me. "Really?"

I sighed, dropped my backpack to the floor, and made my way past him and into the kitchen. "Yes, Dad. We were studying together."

I could hear his heavy footsteps on the hardwood floor. Why was he acting like this? I mean, I know I had just spent the evening with Tyson, but he didn't know that. In all of my life, I'd never given my dad a reason to doubt me. Why was he now?

He sighed as he leaned against the counter and grabbed a banana. "Sorry, Tiny. I guess I'm just agitated." He reached out and patted my shoulder. His signature *I was being a dork and took it out on you* move.

I shrugged, ignoring that tugging in the back of my mind that said he had every right to be suspicious. I had lied. And spent time with a guy he'd forbidden me to see. "I get it. No harm, no foul."

He'd finished his banana, so he leaned over and threw the peel into the garbage. "How's Rebecca?"

I swallowed. Lying once was easy. But the longer I stood here, stringing together more of them, the harder it would be. So I faked a yawn and waved toward the hallway. "She's good. Hey, I'm going to head upstairs and finish my Chem homework and then turn in. Big day of learning tomorrow."

He studied me and then nodded. "Sounds good, peanut. I'll see you in the morning?"

I nodded, pushing all feelings of regret from my mind. I wasn't doing any of this to hurt him. I was trying to help someone. If anything, he should be proud to have a daughter who was so selfless.

When I passed by him, I went up onto my tippy toes and kissed his cheek. "Night, Dad."

He patted me on the back. When I got back out into the hallway, I took the stairs two at a time. I felt as if my head might explode. Lying was a lot of work.

I needed sleep. If I went to bed right now, I'd maybe get six hours.

But when I pulled out my textbooks from my backpack, I realized how much work I actually had to do. It was going to take me into the wee hours of the morning before I finished.

Grabbing my phone, I turned it on. I needed some jams to get through this.

I DON'T KNOW why I thought things were going to change between Tyson and I. Experiencing an intimate moment the night before wasn't enough to suddenly bond us. He was still the same cocky and flirty senior in class the next day.

I spent the whole period watching him text Tammy and flirt with the girl behind us. I wanted to shake him. Heck, I wanted to slap him. What was his problem? Did he only pay attention to me when no one was around?

Thankfully, Ms. Swallow was also watching and was not shy with her warnings. It took a few, but he eventually settled down and focused on the experiment we had been assigned to do.

That only lasted for a few minutes before his phone was out again and he was texting.

Fed up with his behavior, I decided to ignore him and just finish the lab myself. After jotting down the results, the bell rang, and I made my way up to the front. Tyson's complaint was lost in the chatter and movement of students leaving the classroom.

But I didn't care. It was his fault for being a jerk. If he failed this lab, what did it matter to me? I'd pass, and right now, that's all I cared about. Even though my heart felt as if it were breaking a bit inside.

I slipped into the throng of people, hoping to dodge Tyson. Just as I rounded the corner, I felt a hand wrap around my elbow and pull me under the stairs. I yelped, turning to see my assailant.

It was Tyson. I narrowed my eyes. I tried not to glare at him, but I couldn't help it. He was acting like a jerk. I pulled my elbow away and stepped back, pressing my back against the wall.

"What did you need, Tyson?" I asked. I hoped that my voice would come out calm and cool. Not needy and hurt, like I was feeling.

"You ran out of the room." He shoved his hands into his front pockets as he looked over at me. There was a depth to his gaze that caused my breath to catch in my throat.

"I didn't think you noticed." I threaded my thumbs through my backpack straps and studied the speckled tiles below my shoes.

When he didn't respond, I glanced up at him. He was studying me with a small smile on his lips.

"Did I do something?" he asked.

I sighed and glanced out at the students around us. What was I going to say to that? I felt like he was cheating on me, even though I wasn't dating him? Ugh, I could be an idiot sometimes.

"You were just very focused on everything but chemistry. I figured as someone who wants to do well in the class, you'd at least try to pay attention." I dropped my voice. "But you were too interested in flirting with everyone."

Again, he fell silent. Hoping I hadn't just ruined everything, I glanced up to see him watching me. I forced a smile, hoping to let him know that I was cool with everything. I wasn't some needy girl that wanted him to talk to only her.

Gah. When did I become such an emotional basket case?

"I'm sorry," he said, meeting my gaze. "You're right. I was acting like a jerk in there."

I scoffed and glanced around. "I wasn't going to say it, but since you did..."

He laughed. The same way he had in the tree house. It was genuine. And I loved it.

He shook his finger in my direction. "I'm going to have to keep my eye on you, Tiny. You make a guy stand up and give a crap. I like that about you."

I tried to silence my heart as it hammered in my chest. He actually liked something about me. Wow.

"Well, as your tutor, it's my mission to get you through chemistry. If you learn a few life lessons along the way?" I shrugged. "So be it."

He nodded. "So, if I stop getting distracted and help with the labs, you'll promise not to sprint out of class like a bat out of hell?"

I pretended to mull that over. After a few seconds of making him wait, I slowly nodded my head. "Yes. If you try harder, I promise not to leave you in the lurch."

He stuck out his hand and wiggled his fingers. "I swear."

I hesitated before I met his handshake. I tried to ignore the fireworks that exploded across my skin from his touch.

"Good," I said, dropping his hand.

The warning bell rang. We were going to be late if we didn't head to class right now. I shot him one more smile and turned.

"Thanks, Tiny," he said as I started to walk away from him.

There was a tone to his voice that sent shivers up my spine. I stifled a groan when I realized what that meant. I was starting to like Tyson. More than a teenage crush. I was starting to *like him*, like him. This revelation was not going to end well for me.

Instead of dwelling on it, I decided to push the thoughts from my head and walk as fast as I could to Economics. I'd deal with the emotional implications later.

CHAPTER EIGHT

APPARENTLY, the last thing a person should do is stare at their crush all afternoon. Especially if that crush was wearing tight football pants. It was taking all my control not to march across the field and...

I shook my head. I shouldn't finish that thought. I should think of Tyson as a blob. A gelatinous substance I could never have a relationship with. Because that was the truth. I could NEVER have a relationship with Tyson.

I dropped my gaze and toed the grass under my shoe. I needed to focus on something else.

"You feeling okay?" Dad asked from behind me.

I turned to see him with his clipboard in hand, studying me.

Truth was, I was exhausted. From the emotional toll of keeping a secret from Dad—to the emotional rollercoaster I was on every time Tyson touched my hand. It was catching up to me.

"Yeah, I'm not sure. I think I might need to lie down."

Dad nodded. "Good idea. Plus, I don't need you getting my team sick before the big game." He turned his attention to Shorty, who was sitting on the bench. "Shorty, come here and take over."

The poor kid's face drooped as my dad's words registered. Instead of running out onto the field to play with his team, he was going to have to stand by the table and hand out water. I shot him a sympathetic look. I felt for him, but there was no way I wasn't going to leave when given the chance.

"Sure, Boss," he said as he set his helmet down next to him and stood.

I nodded to Dad and made my way over to the school building. Just as I passed the field, I heard my name. Part of me wanted to turn to see if it was Tyson calling after me. But I wasn't sure how I felt about what it meant if it was him and what it meant if it wasn't. So I pushed forward, keeping my head down until I got inside.

In Dad's office, I kept the light off as I pulled a few of his chairs together in a line. Trying hard not to think of all the many behinds that had sat on these chairs, I lay down on top of them and tried to relax. It had already been a long day, and if I was going to help Tyson tonight, it was going to be even longer.

It took some time, but my eyes finally drifted shut and my mind stilled. The only sound I could hear was the ticking of the clock on the wall.

It must have lulled me to sleep because, the next thing I knew, Dad was tapping me on the shoulder. I startled awake, sitting up as I tried to clear my mind.

"You okay?" he asked, raising his eyebrows.

"Yeah. Sorry. I didn't think I'd fall asleep." I turned my head, trying to work out a kink that had formed from sleeping on four chairs that should probably have been thrown away years ago.

He eyed me. "Well, I'm happy you decided to take some time to rest." He walked over to the desk and set his clipboard on it.

I sat up and stretched, glancing toward the hallway outside of his office. "Practice over?"

He grunted a response.

Figuring that I wasn't going to get any more from him, I turned my attention to the clock on the wall.

4:30

I retrieved my phone from my backpack and tried to look relaxed as I scrolled through the messages. My heart stuttered to a stop when I saw I had one from Tyson.

Tyson: I hope you're feeling better. Have to bail tonight. Responsibilities.

I studied his words. For a moment, I let the thought that he was blowing me off for another girl linger, but then I pushed it from my mind. I wasn't going to become that person. I wasn't a crazed jealous girl. Tyson had his life, and I had mine.

Me: Have fun. See you tomorrow.

I hit send and tucked my phone into my backpack. I was actually happy to have a night off. Right now, digesting my feelings and getting a handle on my thoughts sounded better with Tyson not being there.

"You know what I could use?" I asked Dad as I slung my backpack on my shoulder.

He glanced up at me and quirked an eyebrow.

"Shakes and colossal burgers from Ted's."

Dad nodded his approval. "Ooo, haven't been there in a long time." He glanced at his watch. "Give me fifteen minutes, and we can head out."

Ted's Malt Shoppe was a fabulous little place two towns over. It was a place that didn't skimp on anything. I ordered the colossal burger every time, but only could finish half before I wanted to explode. Dad and I started going there after Mom left. Besides our tree house, it was the only other place that was special to just us.

I settled down on one of the chairs and dug into my homework. Before I knew it, Dad was standing over me.

"Ready?"

I nodded, tucked my stuff back into my bag, and followed him out of his office.

Twenty minutes later, he pulled into the small parking

lot of Ted's Malt Shoppe. After parking haphazardly, we
both got out and slammed our doors at the same time. I
smiled. It felt good. I missed hanging out with Dad.

As crazy controlling as he was about my love life, he was
actually a cool guy to spend time with. We'd get to talking
about sports or people-watch, and we'd lose track of time.
We were pretty similar, he and I.

He pulled open the door, and the smell of fried food and
malt powder wafted out. I took in a deep breath, reveling in
the familiarity of this place. Sixties music blared from the
jukebox along the far back wall.

"Well, I'll be." Justine, a waitress who'd hit on my dad
more times than I could count, lowered her order pad. "If it
isn't Josh and Destiny," she said, giving Dad an approving
smile.

"Justine," he said, nodding in her direction.

I watched as his cheeks turned red. Was Dad embarrassed? It'd been a while since we'd come to Ted's, and
maybe I'd never really noticed. But Dad was actually blushing. Weird.

Justine waved her hand toward a trucker in a ball cap,
whose order she was taking, and made her way over to us,
grabbing two menus along the way. "I haven't seen you two
in ages." She eyed Dad, stepping a bit too close to him. "I
thought you moved." She gave him a wink. "Glad to see I
was wrong."

Dad cleared his throat and nodded. "A booth would be

great," he said, stepping aside. I could only assume that if he had his way, he'd be out of this diner as fast as possible.

But I was hungry, and I wasn't going anywhere.

Justine gave him another wink and nodded for us to follow her. Just as we rounded the corner to where the booths were, I stopped.

Ms. Swallow was sitting at the far booth with her head down, reading a book.

"You're right here, honey," Justine said, motioning toward the booth next to us.

I glanced toward where she indicated and then up to Dad.

"Everything okay?" he asked.

I nodded as I slid in. Justine laid the menus in front of us. "My chemistry teacher is here," I said.

Dad coughed and turned. I watched as his gaze landed on Ms. Swallow. He had a strange expression on his face as he turned back to me. "That's the new chemistry teacher?" he asked. His voice seemed forced. Like he was trying to hide something.

Double weird.

I nodded, unfolding the menu. "Yeah."

Justine seemed to have been listening to our conversation because I saw her study Ms. Swallow. "Oh her? That's Ted's niece." She tsked. "Poor thing comes in every night for dinner." She lowered her voice and studied us. "Such a waste. A girl that pretty should be with someone, not alone."

As if she sensed she was being talked about, Ms. Swallow looked up. All three of us snapped our gazes away from her and down to the table.

"I'll have the regular burger and chocolate shake," Dad said folding up his menu and handing it over to Justine.

"Same for me. No onions," I said.

Justine grabbed our menus and nodded. "Got it."

Once she was gone, Dad reached into his front pocket and pulled out a few coins. "Wanna pick some music?" he asked, nodding toward the jukebox.

"Really, Dad? I'm not five." But deep down, I wanted to. I just didn't want to seem too eager. I had the teenage image of not-caring-about-anything to uphold.

Dad studied me. I saw in his gaze that he didn't buy my crap. "Okay," he said as he shrugged and started to scoop up the money.

"Actually, I'd love to." I grabbed the remaining nickels and sprinted from the booth before he changed his mind. As soon as I stepped up to the jukebox, I knew exactly what I was going to play. I loved anything Neil Diamond, but my favorite was *Sweet Caroline*.

After punching in B-7, I tapped my fingers against the glass window as the first notes started. I loved the build up in this song.

"Tiny?"

I jumped. Tyson was standing behind me, wearing a hairnet and apron. My eyes widened. What was happening?

Was I dreaming? It was strange that I would dream about Tyson working at my favorite restaurant. What did that say about me?

"Tyson?" I squeaked. I had half a mind to reach out and see if he was really there.

He glanced around, and for a moment, I thought I saw his cheeks redden. Was he embarrassed that he worked here?

"What—what are you doing here?" He tried to run his hands through his hair, but his fingers just got caught in the holes of the hairnet. As if he suddenly realized that he still had it on, he pulled it from his head and shook his hair out.

"Eating," I said as I was slowly starting to put together the pieces. "Do you work here?"

He hesitated before he nodded.

"So I'm not dreaming."

A slow smile spread across his lips. "You dream about me?"

I snorted and scoffed at the same time, which came out as a choking sound. He raised his eyebrows, and heat raced across my skin.

I was not acting cool about this at all. The only person to blame for my reaction was him. Sneaking up on me like that.

"No," I said. But it was too late. Tyson Blake knew that he was the star of my dreams. I pinched my lips closed. I was scared I would share just how many dreams he'd been a part of.

"I'm sorry I bailed on you. I tried to catch you after practice, but you were with your dad and I didn't want to get you in trouble," he said. He sounded genuine. But that was not what I focused on. It was the one little word, *dad*.

I peeked around him and over to our table. Dad was studying his phone. Thankfully, whatever was on his screen was much more interesting than watching his daughter choose songs.

I grabbed Tyson's arm and pulled him out of view.

"Tiny," he said in that flirty tone that made my stomach flip. "You don't have to manhandle me."

I shot him an exasperated look and dropped my hand, trying to ignore the feeling of his skin against mine. Since when were guys' arms so muscular? I hadn't felt his biceps before, and now I was never going to be able to get that thought from my head.

"My dad is sitting over there," I said in a hushed voice. For some reason, I had thought it was better to drag Tyson into the small hallway where the bathrooms were located. We were now only a foot apart.

Tyson's skin paled as he reached out and opened the door behind me. I couldn't help but stare at him as he got closer. I could smell his soap, and his soft cotton shirt rubbed against my skin. Shivers raced across my body.

"Here," he whispered. His voice was inches from my ear.

My breath caught in my throat. "What?" I asked as I forced myself to turn around. He'd opened a supply closet.

"You want me to go in there? It looks like the opening scene of most murder movies."

He chuckled as he pressed on my lower back. Out of instinct, I moved forward until we were both standing in the closet—inches from each other—and he shut the door. Darkness surrounded me. What was happening?

"Tyson?" I asked, turning with my eyes wide. The only light I saw was the sliver that came in from under the door.

"Sorry." Tyson's voice sent my heart racing. He was so close to me. I couldn't see him, but I could feel him.

Suddenly, the light from a single bulb filled the room. I blinked as spots floated in my vision. "Trying to blind me, Chicken?" I alternated between rubbing my eyes and blinking. I heard a soft chuckle, which caused me to stop. "What?"

He was watching me. "Chicken?"

My cheeks burned when I realized I'd called him by the nickname I'd made up. "Um, yeah." I folded my arms, rubbing my hands against them. This evening was taking the strangest turn.

He stared at me. I hated the way his half smile made me want to confess everything to him. Why was I so weak?

I blew out my breath. "It's your nickname. That way, if my dad looks at my phone, he doesn't know who's texting me." I drew out each word as I studied him. Was he offended? I really thought it was the best for the both of us.

He hesitated. "And Chicken was the best name you could come up with? Not Hercules or Greek God?"

I laughed, which came out more like a snort. "Really? That may be pushing things."

He contorted his face into a sad expression. I rolled my eyes.

"It's Chicken because of your name. You know, Tyson Chicken Nuggets?"

He wrinkled his nose. "Yeah, not a fan of that."

I shrugged and looked around. There were shelves with cleaning supplies and paper products all around us. A mop bucket took up half the floor, which caused Tyson and I to stand close together. I cursed and blessed that thing at the same time.

"It's already on my phone. You can't do anything about it." I shot him a smile.

"That sounds like a challenge."

"Oh, it is." I stopped myself. What was I doing? Was I flirting with Tyson? But he was doing the same to me. Did that mean he was flirting back? Suddenly, I wanted to flee the closet. "So, did you need something from me? Or do you drag all the customers in here?"

He laughed, genuine and unabashed. And I loved it. "I drag all the customers in here." Then his expression grew serious as he studied me.

It must have been the lack of oxygen from standing in a small space with a guy so much taller than me, but I swear he leaned closer. Like, his lips came closer to mine. What was he doing?

He needed to back away. I'd already almost hugged him.

I wasn't sure what I would do if I thought he was leaning in for a kiss.

"I missed talking to you," he said. His voice was low and intentional. Like he knew what he was doing to me. And knowing him, I wasn't surprised.

"We talked this morning."

He shrugged as he reached out to fiddle with something behind me. I swallowed. Was he really doing something or just making an excuse to get closer to me?

As much as I wanted to fight it, I really hoped it was the second reason.

"Talking about chemistry is not the same." He glanced down at me, meeting my gaze. There was something in it. A depth that scared me.

I needed to break this trance he had me in. "How's your mom?"

That did the trick. At the mention of her, his brow furrowed and his eyes darkened. He pulled back. "She's been better."

I didn't realize the amount of body heat Tyson emitted until he pulled away. The room around me felt frigid. As I watched Tyson stiffen, I suddenly realized that mentioning his mom had been a mistake. I hadn't meant to make him upset.

"I'm sorry. I didn't mean to—"

"It's okay, Tiny. I should get back to the kitchen. George will freak out if I'm gone too long." He grabbed his hairnet from his pocket and studied it.

"Oh, okay. I should probably get back as well."

He nodded as he moved his gaze over to me and then ducked his head. Just as he opened the door and stepped out, there was a "humph" from the person he ran into. My heart quickened as I peeked out and saw the wide eyes of Ms. Swallow.

CHAPTER NINE

I WAS AN IDIOT. Why I ever thought I could handle sneaking around with Tyson Blake boggled my mind. I knew we were going to get caught, I just didn't figure it would be by our chemistry teacher.

"Tyson," Ms. Swallow said as her gaze ran over him. Then it fell on me, and her eyebrows rose. "Destiny?" Her brow furrowed. "What were you two doing in there?"

Tyson cleared his throat. "Ms. Swallow," he said as he nodded and slipped past her.

I watched him duck through the swinging door that led to the kitchen. He'd left me alone. With Ms. Swallow. To explain why I had been in a supply closet with a boy. Thanks a lot, Chicken. That nickname matched him more than ever.

"We were..." Why couldn't I think of anything to say? I had the whole English language on the tip of my tongue, but none of it was coming together to form cohesive sentences. "We were..." I cleared my throat. "Um..."

Her eyebrows rose with each failed start.

Thankfully, Dad appeared behind her. Wait. Not thankfully. This was about the worst thing that could ever happen. I glanced at the shelf in front of me and grabbed the first thing I could see. A roll of toilet paper.

"Tiny, why are you in the closet?" he asked.

Ms. Swallow jumped and turned. Thankfully, their meet-cute gave me a second to come up with a plausible story.

"Toilet paper," I said, before anyone else could speak.

I had both of their attention now.

Dad quirked an eyebrow. "What?"

"The bathroom"—I waved toward the door across from the closet—"was out of toilet paper. I figured I'd help a sister out and grab a roll so they weren't stuck to drip dry." I cringed at the fact that I was still talking. I needed to end this conversation and get back to the table, where my mouth would be preoccupied with eating.

"I was just in the bathroom—" Ms. Swallows started.

"So you know how there is a desperate need for toilet paper."

Her eyes widened. I gave her a pleading look. One that I hoped said, *please go along with this,* and not, *I'm a crazy person.*

She studied me then slowly nodded. "Right. Yes. Such a thoughtful thing to do, Destiny."

I pinched my lips together and stepped toward them. "Well, I should probably go put this baby in there." I moved toward the bathroom and slipped inside.

After I splashed water on my face a few times, I patted my skin dry and took a deep breath. So much had happened, and I felt as if my nerves were on fire. It was hard work, sneaking around. But getting to know Tyson made it all worth it.

Once I was cleaned up, I stacked the roll of toilet paper on top of the six-roll tower someone had built. When I got back to the table, I noticed that Dad wasn't alone. Ms. Swallow was there.

When I approached, I saw that they were talking. Dad had a strange expression on his face. Like he was trying to smile, but felt uncomfortable doing it.

"Ms. Swallow is sitting with us?"

Dad nodded. "Yeah. She was alone, so I figured we could keep her company." He snapped his gaze over to me. "That's okay, right?" His voice cracked in a way I'd never heard before.

"Yeah, it's fine. Dad, you okay?" I asked as I paused and tried to figure out where I was supposed to sit. Either by Dad—which felt weird. Or by Ms. Swallow—which felt weirder. So I settled with Dad.

Justine brought our food as soon as my butt hit the bench. I wanted to kiss that woman. People couldn't talk or ask questions about toilet paper or stolen moments in the supply closet with food in their mouths. We would just sit there, chewing.

As all good things, the food eventually came to an end. When both Ms. Swallow and Dad put their napkins down and pushed their plates away, I knew I needed to intervene. I didn't need Dad asking me about the bathroom, and I didn't need Ms. Swallow asking me about Tyson.

"So, your uncle is Ted?" I asked, cringing as I tried to swallow the fry I'd only half chewed.

Ms. Swallow nodded. "That's right. I actually just moved here from Iowa. He's the only person I know."

"Iowa, really?" Dad asked as he leaned forward.

I glanced over at him. Why was he acting like Iowa was the most fascinating place in the world? I wasn't even sure where it was.

They started talking about farms, or the Amish, I wasn't really sure. All I could focus on was the swinging door that Tyson had disappeared through earlier. He was there. On the other side. My heart hammered in my chest.

This wasn't good. It was bad. Really, really bad.

"That is fascinating," Dad said, pulling me from my thoughts. I glanced over to see him smile at Ms. Swallow. "Isn't that fascinating, Destiny?"

"What?" I asked before I bit my lip. I was pretty sure that whatever small talk they were sharing was definitely not fascinating.

"Angelica here was just telling me that the world's largest strawberry is in Iowa."

I stared at him. Was he serious? He was allergic to strawberries. And did he just call Ms. Swallow, Angelica? I was rapidly getting to know more about my teacher than I felt comfortable with. And for some reason, I was sensing this attraction vibe—at least from Dad—and it made my skin crawl.

My mind really couldn't process what was happening, so I did the only thing I seemed to be good at lately, I lied.

"That is interesting. For someone who can eat strawberries."

Ms. Swallow's eyebrows rose as she moved her gaze from me to Dad.

He coughed, and I swear he purposely kicked me under the table. Or Ms. Swallow has a spastic leg. Whichever it was, I winced as pain shot up my leg.

"I'm allergic," Dad said as if he were apologizing.

Ms. Swallow's cheeks hinted red as she nodded. "Oh, I'm sorry."

Dad laughed. "Yeah, if I eat one—" he expanded his hands out from his cheeks to signify his face exploding.

"That's terrible," Ms. Swallow said, taking a sip of her water.

They both nodded, and a strange silence fell around them.

This was weird, and it made me very uncomfortable. Dad was a strict *love only breaks your heart and leaves you lonely* kind of guy. Watching him turn all schoolboy over Ms. Swallow was like watching an alien hijack his body.

I needed to get away. Only thing was, moony-boy was my ride.

I shoved the last fry into my mouth and turned to him. "Ready to go, Dad? I got homework to do." I slid out of the booth and stood.

Ms. Swallow grabbed her purse and shouldered it. "Yeah, I should get going."

Dad nodded as he followed after me. "Yeah. Big day tomorrow. Game day."

Ms. Swallow nodded as she tucked a strand of her strawberry blonde hair behind her ear. "I love high school football. Much better than the professional leagues. Wins mean more when it's your school."

I stared at her dumbfounded. Was there a "How to Woo Joshua Davis" book out there somewhere? How did she know exactly what she needed to say to make Dad fall for her? From the slack-jaw look he had, it was working.

"That's exactly what I say," he said as he extended his arm for her to follow him.

Well, I guess we are walking Ms. Swallow to her car. Yippee.

They kept talking at the register and out into the parking lot. They stood awkwardly next to her car as they finished talking about...something. I'd stopped listening at cow tipping.

Finally, I got tired of standing there as the third wheel, walked over to our car, and climbed in. A few minutes later, Dad appeared and pulled the driver's door open.

"Hey, Tiny?" he asked as he ducked his head down.

"Yep," I said, straightening in my seat.

"Mind if we give Angelica a ride home? She tried to start her car, but I think the ignition died. She's going to leave it here and has no way home."

Great. More awkward flirting.

But I wanted Dad to be happy, so I nodded. "Sure."

For some reason, it felt weird to ride up front, so I offered my seat to Ms. Swallow. She objected at first, but I wouldn't take no for an answer and climbed into the back.

Dad started the car, and their conversation continued. Not wanting to eavesdrop on them, I pulled out my phone and stared at Tyson's number. After our interaction in the closet, I felt more comfortable texting him. And if I were honest, I missed talking to him.

So I found his number and pressed the message button.

Me: Wanna hear something weird?

I waited. And then felt stupid. He wasn't going to answer. He was at work. But then my phone chimed and his message appeared.

Tyson: Always

I smiled. I could hear his voice in my head as I read his words. This was not good, but I couldn't help myself. I liked Tyson Blake.

Me: My dad and Ms. Swallow are currently flirting like teenagers

His message came faster this time.

Tyson: Really? The Boss has a heart?

I stared at it. Did he really just call my dad heartless?

Tyson: That was a stupid answer. Let me try again. Wow, how did that happen?

Good. He realized how bad that had sounded. It was nice that he was picking up on things like that.

Me: We ran into her at Ted's. Apparently he's her uncle?

Tyson: Oh that's why she's always eating here. I just figured she liked her grease with a side of fries.

I chuckled as I glanced up at Dad and Ms. Swallow, who were still engrossed in conversation.

Me: You won't believe what he calls her. Angelica. That's weird, huh? Teachers being called by their first names.

Tyson: Totally weird.

This was fun. I loved that I could talk to Tyson, and Dad was so preoccupied that I didn't have to worry about him noticing.

Me: How's work?

Was it wrong that I wanted to know more about him?

Tyson: I work with George. I'm pretty sure he's as old as dirt.

I laughed.

Tyson: Get this, he doesn't really talk, he grunts. One grunt means, get out of my way. Two grunts means, you're burning something.

Three grunts means, stop talking, I'm watching my show. It's a great system.

I nodded as I typed my response.

Me: Sounds amazing. I'll have to keep that in mind for our next study session. I know the big game is tomorrow. Will Saturday work?

I hit send and waited for his response. When it didn't come right away, I worried I'd offended him. Was it wrong to suggest studying over the weekend? He probably had a much more happening social life than I did. A movie and a bucket of popcorn was my Saturday night.

Before I got his answer, Dad pulled up in front of a small yellow house and shifted the car into park. Ms. Swallow turned and smiled at the both of us.

"Thanks so much for the ride, Josh"—ugh, that was weird—"and Destiny, I'll see you in class tomorrow."

I saluted her with two fingers, and she climbed out of the car.

Dad leaned over before she could shut the door and said, "I'll see you at the teacher's lounge for coffee."

Ms. Swallow nodded and slammed the door.

I stared at him. Whoa. "Smooth, Dad."

He shot me a look before we drove off. "What does that mean, Tiny?"

Was he really going to make me say it? "Um, was I the only one in the car? You couldn't stop talking to my chemistry teacher. You literally never drew breath. I mean, it was world record worthy."

He sighed. The one that said he was annoyed with me. "I did not, Tiny. I was just making pleasant conversation, that's all. It wouldn't hurt you to do the same."

I wanted to snort. I wanted to tell him that he was delusional, but I was tired and ready to be done for the night. So I said, "Fine." And settled into my seat for the five-minute drive home.

It wasn't until I'd changed into my pajamas and crawled under my covers that my phone chimed. My heart picked up speed as I reached over and grabbed it from my nightstand.

It was from Tyson.

Tyson: Sorry, Tiny. Won't work. I'm booked that day.

I flopped back on my bed, burying my phone under some pillows. All the excitement I'd felt about spending more time with Tyson came crashing down around me. He had something else going on. My assumption about his active social life was true.

He was always going to be the popular jock, and I would be the outcast dweeb. It's literally written in the by-laws.

And never the two shall meet.

CHAPTER TEN

I GOT to Ms. Swallow's class early the next day. I wanted to catch her and ask her to not say anything to my dad about Tyson and I and our closet rendezvous.

But she wasn't there.

I waited at her desk until the bell rang. All the kids had gathered at their lab tables before I gave up and headed to sit in my spot. Where Tyson also wasn't.

What was happening? Why was everyone missing?

Ms. Swallow's heels could be heard as she entered the room. Her cheeks were flushed, and she was carrying a mug of coffee. Suddenly, her coffee date with Dad floated into my mind.

Of course. She was seeing Dad. Ugh. Had they been flirting?

Memories of the night before came rushing back. Blegh.

Adults shouldn't be allowed to flirt. It comes across awkward and creepy.

"Good morning, class," she said, setting her mug down and pushing her hair from her face. She looked different today. She had on makeup.

This was getting worse.

Tyson appeared in the doorway, and I almost celebrated. Finally, something to take my mind off Dad and Ms. Swallow.

But as soon as I took in his countenance, a worried feeling brewed in my gut. Something was wrong.

"Do you have a slip, Mr. Blake?" Ms. Swallow asked, reaching out her hand and wiggling her fingers.

Tyson ducked his head as he walked past her. "No," he said. His voice was low.

A frustrated expression passed over Ms. Swallow's face. "Excuse me, Mr. Blake. That's a tardy. Three tardies and I'll have to send you to detention."

He shrugged as he dropped his backpack next to our table and sat. He kept his gaze focused on the table in front of him.

Ms. Swallow gave him one more disapproving look before she turned to the board and began writing. I wanted to ask Tyson what was wrong. I wanted to tell him that I was here for him. I wanted to do...something.

But he never looked my way. Instead, he pulled out his phone and started playing some candy game on it. I sighed as I turned my attention back to Ms. Swallow.

No matter how hard I tried, I couldn't keep my focus from shifting back over to Tyson. What was the matter? Did it have to do with his mom? So many questions floated around in my mind, and I didn't realize until the bell rang that class was over.

I stared down at my paper covered with a bunch of doodles and one sentence of notes.

Bromine and Mercury. Liquid at room temperature.

Was that what the lesson had been about? Honestly, I had no idea.

Tyson was gone when I glanced back up. The need to catch up with him raced through my mind, so I grabbed my backpack and shoved my notebook into it as I made my way across the room.

"Destiny?" Ms. Swallow stopped me as she stepped into my path.

I wanted to groan, but instead I glanced over at her. "Yeah?"

She looked nervous. Why was she nervous?

"I just wanted to make sure that we're okay. Last night, I did not mean to monopolize the time you were spending with your dad."

I peeked past her, hoping to see Tyson walk down the hall. No such luck. I needed to get out there before the throng of students swallowed him up.

"It's fine. I'm happy you two are getting along."

She continued as if I hadn't spoken. "It's just been hard, me not knowing anyone here. Your father has been so nice to me. And then yesterday, it was really nice that you guys allowed me to join in."

This conversation was never going to end. I glanced over at her. "I'm happy for you. But I should really get to class."

It seemed as if she'd suddenly remembered that she'd cornered me in her room. Her cheeks turned red as she stepped aside. "Yes. Sorry. You're free to go."

I nodded and moved toward the door. But then the reason I'd come into class so early rushed back to me. "Could you do me a favor?"

Her eyes lit up. "Sure. Anything."

"Can you not tell my dad that you put me and Tyson together as lab partners. Or that you saw us in the closet at Ted's?"

Her brow furrowed. Did she really need to think this hard about it?

She hesitated and then nodded. "Sure. It'll be between you and me."

I smiled and continued out the door, calling, "Thank you," behind me.

Now out in the hall, my hopes deflated. Tyson was gone. There was no way I was going to catch up to him now. Blast Ms. Swallow and her need to tell me her whole life story.

I threaded my thumbs through the straps of my backpack and ducked my head. Might as well head to English.

Just as I passed the lunchroom, a hand reached out and grabbed my arm, pulling me into a supply closet. I yelped and tried to break free—until I saw it was Tyson.

He shut the door, flipped on the light, and glanced over at me. He still looked upset.

"Is this going to be a habit of yours? Forcing me into closets?" I asked as he studied me. Butterflies erupted in my stomach when I met his gaze. There was something there that I couldn't quite read but made me desperate to know what he was thinking.

He laughed, glancing to the side and then back over at me. When his gaze returned, there was an intensity to it that caused my breath to catch in my throat. He was going through something, and I couldn't figure it out. I cared about Tyson, and seeing him this upset affected me in a way that I couldn't describe.

"What's wrong?" I asked.

Before I could react, he crossed the room and slipped his hands around my waist. My heart pounded as I glanced up at him. This whole closet-thing was rapidly becoming my favorite move ever.

"What are you doing?" I asked, my voice coming out breathy.

"Something I've wanted to do for a while now." Just as the last words left his lips, he dipped down and pressed them against mine.

Fireworks exploded across my skin at every point of contact. It only took a second for me to get over the shock and respond. At first, I was nervous. What if I did it wrong? What if I bit him? Suddenly, I was Porter in our second-grade kiss debacle. Why had I been so critical of him?

Thankfully, Tyson had experience. He pulled me closer and deepened the kiss. His lips moved against mine as if he were looking for something. I responded, forcing out all my thoughts of inadequacy and losing myself in the moment.

I allowed my hands to slide up his chest and up to his shoulders. I could feel every muscle twitch as I moved across them. When I reached his hair, I let my fingers play with each strand.

And just as quickly as it started, he pulled back. A look of pain flashed in his eyes. "I'm sorry, Destiny," he said as he grabbed his backpack and moved toward the door. "You deserve better." He met my gaze for a moment, before he dropped it. "Just forget I did this, okay?"

He paused, as if waiting for me to answer. The only rational thing I could do was lie. It was the only thing I seemed to be able to do lately.

So I opened my puffy lips and said, "Of course."

He pulled open the door and left.

I stood in the middle of the supply closet, not really understanding what had happened.

Tyson Blake had kissed me. *Me.*

I stumbled over to an overturned bucket and sat down. I placed my head between my knees and took a deep breath—just as my elementary school nurse had told me to do when I felt overwhelmed.

How did that happen? And why?

I sat up and grabbed my phone. I needed Rebecca.

After texting her to meet me, I placed my head back

onto my knees and took deep breaths. A few minutes later, there was a knock on the door and it opened.

"Des?" Rebecca asked as she peeked her head into the room.

I sat up and nodded. "Yeah. I'm in here."

She entered, letting her gaze sweep across the room. "Yeah. I got that. But why are you in here?"

I motioned to the bucket next to me, and she complied by sitting. Once she was comfortable, I told her all about Tyson being at Ted's. About Dad and Ms. Swallow. And then the kiss. A lot about the kiss.

The air fell silent as the last words left my lips. I watched as her eyebrows rose. I could tell she was trying to digest what I had said. I didn't blame her. It was a lot of information.

"Wow," she said, leaning back on the wall behind her. "He kissed you?"

I nodded as I reached up and touched my lips. That was one thing I was sure of. I had definitely kissed Tyson. Well, actually, Tyson had kissed me. And it wasn't some lame kissing booth at the school fair or a dare given to him by his teammates. He had met me in a dark closet, where there was no one around...

I glanced around. Was Tyson embarrassed by me?

No. That couldn't be it. I was sure that Dad was the reason he wanted to hide our relationship.

Ugh.

Why did I keep saying we were in a relationship?

And then a sour feeling formed in my stomach. We were in a sort of strange relationship. I had come to know so much about Tyson. And they weren't things that revolved around chemistry. I knew about his life. I'd seen his mom. I wondered how many of his teammates knew about what he was struggling with.

Probably none.

"This is..." Rebecca paused as if she were trying to come up with a good description. I turned to look at her, hoping she'd give me some amazing advice. "This is amazing. Des, you two are really cute together."

That was the last thing I needed to hear. There was nothing amazing about our relationship. We could never be together. Ever. I was pretty sure Dad would ground me and kick Tyson off the team if he found out what I'd done.

But none of that scared me as much as the fact that Tyson had asked me to forget the kiss. That definitely didn't scream happily-ever-after. He regretted his decision to kiss me. He regretted me.

"But he asked me to forget it, Bec." I leaned against the wall and blew out my breath. Even speaking the words out loud hurt. Like, boa constrictor around my heart hurt. How had everything gone south so fast? "That doesn't really make me confident about the meaning of the kiss."

I heard her sigh. "It's probably just complicated. I've been hearing rumors from some of the other cheerleaders that his home life is pretty rocky. That's why he's been showing up to practice just drained."

I glanced over at her. I knew exactly what she was talking about. I'd witnessed it first hand.

"Like what things?" I asked, just to make sure that we were talking about the same thing.

Rebecca shrugged and picked some lint off her miniskirt. "His mom is drinking again, which makes it hard for his little sister." She glanced over at me. "He's been having some of the other cheerleaders help out with watching Cori." She narrowed her eyes. "He hadn't told you any of this?"

Told me, no. I only knew about it because he had to pick his mom up when he was driving me home. Our supposed relationship was probably all made up in my mind. He was just being nice. That was all. Tyson Blake didn't have feelings for me. I'd imagined them and then obsessed about them.

"I'm such an idiot," I said, closing my eyes and tipping my face toward the ceiling.

I felt Rebecca's hand rest on mine. "You're not an idiot. He kissed you, Des. That means something." I glanced over at her and fought the tears that formed on my lids. She shot me a sympathetic look. "Give him some time."

I sighed and grabbed my backpack. I was late for class, and so was Rebecca. She was probably right. I needed to give him some time. A break from the questions forming in my mind seemed like a good idea too.

I needed to focus on school and Pep Group. And I was going to start right now.

We stood and left the closet. I said goodbye to Rebecca and walked down the now-empty halls to class. With each step, I forced my mind to clear. I wasn't going to let Tyson occupy my thoughts anymore. I was going to be strong and move on.

Or I was going to die trying.

CHAPTER ELEVEN

THANKFULLY, Dad felt it was more important for me to man the Pep Group booth than the water table for the big game. He'd assigned Shorty to that detail. And I was grateful. Standing on the sidelines, watching Tyson run around, was not how I wanted to spend my Friday evening.

After all, we hadn't seen each other since our closet kiss, and I'd done a pretty good job keeping him from my mind. I only thought about him once every five minutes. It wasn't great, but I was getting better.

I stood at the table, taking putting out foam fingers and pennants on a stick. Dad had gone all out for the first game. He always said wins are accomplished with two ingredients. First, the players. Second, the support. If people are cheering for the team, they play better. Both are needed to clinch the victory.

"Hey, Destiny."

I turned to see Samson and Jessica walking up to the table. They seemed pretty chummy lately. I eyed how close their arms were to each other. Had they started something?

I forced down the groan that clung to my throat. That was the last thing I needed. Watching two lovestruck people figure out their attraction for each other. But instead of focusing on that, I put them to work.

The game started in an hour, and people were beginning to show up to claim their seats.

Once I set up Samson at the cash box and Jessica with the bags, I told them I was going to grab a soda and be right back. They nodded, and I made my way over to the concession stand.

I settled on a Sprite and a pretzel. As I made my way back to our booth, I noticed that Samson and Jessica seemed very engrossed in their conversation. Not wanting to interrupt, I walked behind the bleachers and stopped at the back stairs.

No one was around. This was perfect. I brushed a stair clean with my hand and sat down. Ten minutes alone seemed like heaven.

I bit off a chunk of pretzel and stared at the chain-link fencing in front of me. I allowed my mind to wander as I chewed.

"Come here often?"

I jumped and turned, my heart pounding in my chest. Of course, fate and its cruel sense of humor. Tyson was standing a few feet off in his football get up. He had his eyebrows raised and an uneasy expression on his face.

I brushed off my lips, hoping there weren't any crumbs, and nodded. How was I supposed to handle this? My gaze dropped to his lips. The memory of them pressed against mine raced through my thoughts.

Stupid memory.

"Yeah," I said, finally finding my voice. "I like being alone."

Ugh. How lame did I sound? *I like being alone?* Who says that?

Tyson ran his hands through his hair. "I get it. That's why I come here."

I chewed my lip and nodded. When I saw his gaze move down my face, I wondered for a moment if he was remembering our kiss too.

He took a step closer to me, and my heart responded. I blew out my breath slowly, hoping it would calm the butter-flies in my stomach.

"I'm sorry about what happened earlier." He dropped his gaze to the ground. I wondered why he wouldn't look at me.

Was he ashamed that he kissed me? Embarrassed?

The more I thought about it, the more I realized that I really didn't want to hear the answer to those questions. I wasn't sure I could handle the truth either way.

So I forced a smile. "No worries. It's totally fine." I leaned forward hoping what I was about to say next would come out silly instead of creepy. "Not the first time that's ever happened." Except it was.

He eyed me. "You've kissed a lot of guys in closets."

I made a *pssh* sound. "Yeah."

I could tell from the look on his face that he wasn't sure if he believed me or not. But then he nodded, and that blasted half-smile returned. "I'm impressed, Tiny."

I shrugged and leaned back, resting my elbow on the stair above me. My conversation with Rebecca earlier rushed back to me. I was a little hurt that he never told me that he had a little sister. Before I could filter my words, I blurted out, "So you have a little sister?"

Tyson shifted. "Have you been stalking me?"

My lips parted as I tried to figure out a witty comeback to that. But nothing came, so I decided to own it. "Bec told me that you've been having some cheerleaders help you watch her."

He pushed his hands through his hair. "Yeah. Tammy. Her little sister goes to school with Cori, and she helps out when I have practice and my mom..." A pained expression passed over his face.

Seeing him hurt made my chest squeeze. "I'm sorry." I knew all too well the pain that came from a flaky parent.

He shrugged and kicked a rock with his shoe. "It's no biggie." He glanced up, and a forced smile spread across his lips. "I've got it handled."

"Is that why you were brooding this morning?" Heat raced to my cheeks.

He quirked an eyebrow. "Brooding? I was brooding?"

I nodded, like that was a totally normal way to describe someone.

"Yeah, then that's why I was brooding. Mom couldn't get up this morning, so I had to take Cori to school. Elementary starts an hour later than us, and I had to find someone who'd let me drop her off so I could make it to Chem before the bell rang." He scrubbed his face. "As you could see, I failed at that too."

I studied him, and sympathy washed over me. It wasn't fair that he had this much responsibility dumped on his shoulders. So I gave him an encouraging smile. "You're doing great. Cori's lucky to have you."

He nodded and then glanced over to the large scoreboard where the clock shone against the setting sun. "Yeesh. Gotta go. Told the Boss I had to run to my car to grab my jock—" He stopped and pinched his lips together. "Sorry."

Heat raced across my whole body, and I prayed that he wouldn't notice.

"Anyway, I should go before I say anything more incriminating."

I nodded and waved him away. "Be gone. Before my dad finds out we've been talking and forces you to play without your jockstrap." I pinched my lips together and gave him a look that I hoped said, oh yeah, I went there.

He shot me a smile, appreciating my attempt at humor and turned away. Just before he was out of earshot, he glanced back at me. "Thanks, Tiny."

I did a mini bow, and by the time I looked up, he was gone.

I ate the rest of my pretzel, sitting there, thinking about our conversation. About Tyson. I felt bad for him. He had his sister and his mom to worry about. And me? I had an overprotective dad who cared about me. Who didn't get wasted at some bar and force me to pick him up. As much as I complained about how Dad treated me, I was lucky. And I wanted to remember that.

I put my napkin in the empty tray, grabbed my Sprite, and headed over to the booth. Samson and Jessica were still deep in conversation, and I doubted they even noticed me when I walked up. I said hi and everything, but they didn't look at me.

I blew a loose strand of hair from my face and sighed. Well, this was going to be fun.

BY HALFTIME, we'd sold out of foam fingers and Panther visors. Dad was going to be happy. Well, partially happy. When he found out what some of the students decided to do with the foam fingers, he was going to blow a gasket. But it was a high school football game, what did he expect?

When the cheerleaders ran out onto the field, I stood and started shifting the product around to make it look like we had more things than we did. Samson and Jessica had gone off for a snack, leaving me alone.

"Wow, Destiny. This is amazing."

I turned to see Ms. Swallow standing next to the table with an appreciative look on her face. I raised my eyebrows. "Really?"

She nodded—maybe a bit too enthusiastically. I quirked an eyebrow but didn't say anything. I tried not to wonder if the reason she was talking to me was because of my dad. I scoffed. That was stupid. She was my teacher. Liking my dad was not a prerequisite for talking to me.

"Yeah. I really like your school spirit."

I shrugged as I filled the cup that held the banners. "It's the only group that my dad will let me join. Plus, he's really pushing for us to go to state this year and 'fans are just as important as players.' " I attempted my best Dad voice.

When I glanced over at Ms. Swallow, she was smiling at me. Maybe a little too much.

Stop thinking like that, Tiny.

But I couldn't help it. This was too weird. Seeing a person actually *like* Dad? Bile built up in my throat, so I pushed all thoughts of Dad dating from my mind.

It was really ridiculous if I broke it down in my mind. Dad had told me that relationships and love were useless from the moment Mom left. The only way to keep yourself safe was to keep everyone at a distance. So even allowing those ideas of him dating was crazy.

No. The only reason Ms. Swallow was talking to me was because I was the Pep Group President and she wanted to buy some physical school support.

"Did you want to get something? We're out of foam fingers and panther visors."

Her eyes widened as she glanced at the remaining paraphernalia on the table. "Um, yeah, sure. I'll take a banner and..." She ran her finger through the air as she pointed to all the items. "A panther t-shirt."

I grabbed her items and stuffed them into a bag. "That's thirty dollars."

Her eyes widened, but she nodded, pulling her purse forward and getting out her wallet. After she paid, she stayed by the table. I eyed her. Was it rude for me to ask her to leave?

After I helped an enthusiastic grandmother and a man with a t-shirt that could barely cover his stomach, Samson and Jessica came back. I declared that it was my break time and slipped from the booth. Ms. Swallow must have grown bored watching me or sensed that I wanted to be left alone, because she melded into the crowd that was making its way back to the stand in anticipation of the start of the second half.

I made my way over to the fence that lined the field and leaned against it. As much as I hated that Dad forced me to help out with the football team, I really loved the feeling of game day. The anticipation. The excitement. It surrounded the stadium in a cloud of school spirit.

I stayed at the fence, watching the game until after the third quarter. I probably took a longer break than I should have, but Samson and Jessica didn't seem to notice me when I was there, so I doubted they noticed when I was gone.

When I got back, they asked if they could be done for the night, and I nodded, waving them away with my hand. Very little sales were made in the last quarter anyway.

A cheer rose up as the Panthers scored to end the game. I smiled as I started packing the boxes with the remaining items. Dad would be in a good mood. The first game always made him nervous. He felt it set the mood for the rest of the season.

I made a few more sales from overly excited parents who seemed to want to remember this night and the victory. By the time I had everything put away, there were only the detention students wandering around, picking up garbage with skewers.

I folded down the table and slammed it shut.

"How'd we do?" Dad asked as he walked up to me.

I straightened and shot him a smile. "Good. Sold over half the items."

Dad couldn't fight his grin anymore. "What a great night, huh?" He turned and looked lovingly at the field.

"Want me to go so you can get a room?"

Dad turned and shot me a look. "Nice."

I shrugged and folded up the second table. "You were getting all goo-goo eyes."

He reached out and tousled my hair. "You know I only have eyes for my little girl."

I glanced over at him. Was that true? I wanted to know

what he thought about Ms. Swallow. Was it possible for him to have feelings for her?

"Ms. Swallow stopped by." I studied him. Waiting for some incriminating expression that would tell me what he thought of her.

"Angelica? Really?"

His face didn't change. Man, he was good.

He nodded. "That's nice. The players need to see that their teachers support them. I'm happy she came."

Okay, this wasn't working. I needed to be more direct. "She was asking about you."

He motioned toward the boxes, and I began stacking them in his arms. His expression didn't falter. "That makes sense. I am the coach. I come up in most conversations about the football team."

I sighed. This was pointless. I set the rest of the boxes on the flatbed cart that I'd hidden under the tables. After I laid the tables on top, we both made our way over to the school.

Football players began filtering out of the building as we approached. Just as we got to the doors, Rebecca came out. Her cheeks were pink, and her ponytail bounced around as she talked to another cheerleader.

"Des," she said when she saw me. She said goodbye to the other girl and made her way over.

"Great routines," Dad said as he leaned against the open door.

"Thanks, Mr. D." She glanced over at me. "So, there's an after-party, and I was wondering if Destiny could come.

After all, she's done so much to help the team. She should be there."

Heat raced to my cheeks as I glanced over at Dad. He had his brow furrowed as he studied us. I could see the indecisiveness in his gaze. He liked Rebecca. He thought she was a good influence on me. But a party meant boys.

"Don't worry, I know the rules. It's strictly a girl party," she said as if she read my dad's mind.

That seemed to appease him. "Oh, then sure. She can go." He glanced over to the flatbed. Just as he finished speaking, Shorty came into view carrying the water jug and table. "Shorty, help bring these things in."

Shorty glanced from Dad over to me. I could see the frustration in his eyes. But, he just nodded, dumped the water table items on the cart, and wheeled it into the school.

I turned to Rebecca with my lips parted. I couldn't believe that Dad had actually agreed to this. "I'll grab my stuff from my locker and meet you at your car."

CHAPTER TWELVE

I STOOD on the sidewalk waiting for Rebecca to pull up. It didn't take long for her beat-up Malibu to come sputtering around the corner and park next to the curb.

I opened the side door and got inside. Once I was buckled in, she drove off.

"Where's this party?"

She glanced over at me. "At Brutus's house."

I stared at her. "What? Why is there a girl-only party at Brutus's house?"

She gave me a sideways look, and realization passed over me. "Oh. You lied," I said.

She shrugged and merged onto the main road. "Sue me."

"I'm just impressed, that's all."

"Come on, Des. Don't make me feel bad about this. Your dad is crazy overprotective. You should be able to experience the high school life."

I stared at her like she had two heads. "Um, who are you, and what did you do with my best friend."

Her cheeks turned red as she studied the road. "What are you talking about? I'm the same."

There was a change in her voice that told me she was lying to me too. "Okay, you need to spill. What's going on?"

She sighed as she settled back in her seat. "Remember how I asked you about Colten?" Her gaze slipped over to me before she moved it back to the road.

"Yeah," I said, drawing out the word.

"Well, I might have met him at the Jordan carnival last night." She pinched her lips.

"And?" I prodded.

"And we may have kissed."

There were no words. "You kissed Colten?" How could my straight-A, church-going, perfect best friend get caught up with the school delinquent.

But, from the elated expression on her face, I could tell that she was happy. Who was I to judge? So I grinned. "That's great, Bec. I'm happy for you."

She sighed. It sounded relaxed. "He said he might come to the party tonight. Bringing you was a little selfish on my part. I kind of needed a wing woman."

"Sounds like you're landing a guy no problem," I said, glancing out the window. What I would give to be her right now. A guy liked her. And she liked him back. It seemed so simple.

She giggled. It was high-pitched. "I am not landing, Colten."

"You kissed, Bec. Guys don't normally do that with girls they don't like." Except for me. Apparently, guys kiss me and then ask me to forget it. I tucked a strand of hair behind my ear.

"Tyson will be there."

My stomach turned. Why hadn't I realized that? I shook my head. I hadn't thought about it because my best friend had lied and said this was a girl-only party. And Tyson was most certainly not a girl.

"Yeah, I'm not sure I want that." The memory of our awkward conversation before the game came flooding back. Sure, we left things on a positive note, but that didn't mean I wanted to see him. And definitely not when I was in my sweaty clothes.

"What? Come on, you'll be fine."

I scoffed. "Bec, look at me. I'm not in party attire. And I definitely don't want Tyson to see me all sweaty."

She eyed me and then flipped on her blinker. "Come on, you can shower and change at my house, and then we'll head over."

"Bec—"

"It'll be fun. Besides, we don't want to be the first people there."

I pinched my lips together. There was no way I was going to talk her out of this, so I settled back in my seat. If I was going to be forced to go to this party, I might as well look good.

───────

THE PARKING at Brutus's house was crazy. Rebecca had to park two streets away, and then we had to walk. What would have been no problem in my Converses felt like a marathon in the heels Rebecca had insisted I wear with the red dress she'd loaned me.

I sighed as I pulled at the A-line skirt that flowed around my legs. I felt like an imposter. This whole outfit wasn't me. I was flats and calf-length skirts. This dress hit just above my knee and made me uncomfortable. I was never listening to Rebecca again.

We walked up the driveway—past the seniors pressed against a nearby car, making out—and I shot Rebecca a look. She shrugged as she gave me a hopeful smile. "Come on, Des. This will be fun."

I'd heard "Come on, Des" so much tonight that I was starting to think it was my full name. I sighed and nodded. I needed to stop complaining and just focus on the task at hand. Get Colten to notice Rebecca. Having a job to do calmed me down and focused my attention.

"Okay, I promise, no more complaining. Let's find Colten so we can get out of here."

She wrapped an arm around my shoulders and squeezed me. "That's the friend I know and love."

I shot her a look. "You owe me."

"Got it."

We walked through the open door, and music blared from the speakers. People were standing every few feet, talking in clusters of sweaty, flirty bodies. As I walked past a particularly inebriated group, one stepped back and landed on my foot.

I yelped and smacked his shoulder. When it became apparent that he wasn't going notice me, I shoved him, and he toppled forward into the crowd around him.

Worried for my safety, I left Rebecca, who was doing some recon with other groups, and made my way out the back door and onto the deck. There was more space out here. Some people were in the pool—fully clothed—others were sitting on the deck furniture or making out next to trees.

I shivered as I thought about the amount of germs that were being swapped. Suddenly, I didn't feel so upset that Dad forbade me from coming to parties. It was just a giant hook-up place. I shook my head. Not for me.

I glanced around, hoping I'd be able to spot someone to talk to. Rebecca must have found Colten 'cause she didn't text to ask me where I'd wandered off to. At least my best friend was having a good time.

As I scanned the other side of the pool, my gaze landed on Tyson. He was standing in a circle with other football players, laughing. He looked so at home. What a stark contrast to me. This was not where I belonged.

His gaze found its way over to me. Embarrassed, I dropped my eyes and focused on the wood slats of the deck. Did he notice me? Would he come over?

Thoughts burned in my mind as I tried to calm down. He was in his element. I doubted that the captain of the football team would break from his group to talk to me. I was a closet-and-behind-the-stadium friend. And I was okay with that. I didn't want Dad to find out we'd ever spoken. Right?

"You came."

Tyson's smooth, playful voice filled the air around me. Had he said that to me? I took a deep breath—preparing myself for disappointment—and glanced up.

Up at Tyson's smile as he studied me.

Yep. He'd been talking to me. He'd actually broken off from his friends and come over to me. *Me.*

As much as I tried to push down my excitement, I couldn't help it. I was on cloud nine.

"Yep," I said, shrugging as if this wasn't some miracle.

"Wow. Your dad let you?"

I chewed my lip. Should I rat Rebecca out? Well, she was living fast and loose, hanging with the bad boy of the school. So I shrugged. "Bec told him it was a girl-only party."

Tyson nodded. "Nice. I have a little more respect for Rebecca now." His gaze slipped down to my lips and I wondered if he was thinking about our closet encounter or if I had something on my face.

It probably wasn't the kiss, so I tried to nonchalantly bring up my hand and rub my mouth. "So, you're here."

He laughed and glanced around. "Yeah. Got a sitter for Cori. She was asleep anyway." His expression turned serious as he glanced down at me.

My heart soared from the fact that he felt comfortable enough to tell me about her. "That's sweet. You're a good brother."

He shoved his hands into his front pockets. "She's a cutie. It's hard not to want to take care of her."

I nodded. "It's true," I muttered under my breath before I realized what I'd just said.

He leaned forward as if he were trying to catch my words. "What? What's true?"

I turned slightly, not wanting to answer that question. "Nothing."

He reached out, wrapping his arm around my waist and pulling me closer. It was a totally innocent and flirty move, but it sent my heart racing and memories rushing back to me. The feeling his lips on mine. The heat of his skin against me.

When I glanced up at him, I saw that his expression had grown serious. He'd felt something too.

He dropped his arm and stepped away. "Sorry. Um, I didn't mean to do that."

I laughed, hoping it sounded natural and not forced like it felt. "It's fine." Why did he keep saying that? *I didn't mean to.* Why did touching me always have to end in an apology? It was hard to admit, but it hurt.

"It's okay," I said, straightening out my skirt.

He pushed his hands through his hair. "Can I get you a drink?"

I felt so parched, I was a second away from jumping into the pool. "Sure."

He nodded and started to walk off before he turned. "Anything in particular?"

I shook my head. "Just no alcohol."

"Yeah. I stay away from that stuff, too."

Of course he did. With his mom, I didn't blame him.

It didn't take him long to return with two water bottles. He handed one over to me, and I took it. After drinking half the bottle, I glanced over at him. He had a smile on his lips.

"What?"

"You were thirsty."

"It's from standing in the sun, selling all that team spirit at the game." I pointed my finger at him and jabbed his chest.

He winced and reached up, catching my fingers. When he realized it, he dropped my hand and parted his lips.

"Don't," I said.

He glanced at me. "Don't?"

"Stop apologizing for touching me. It's making me feel like you're a kid in a china store. I won't break." I met his gaze with all the force I could muster.

He laughed and raised his hands. "Wow. Tiny, you're

more forceful than I imagined." He leaned forward until he was inches from my ear. "Is it wrong if I say I like it?"

Shivers raced through my back and exploded throughout my body. Realizing he needed an answer, I shook my head. "It's always okay to tell a girl that she's strong and independent."

He pulled back to stare down at me. "And that's you." His gaze turned serious as his expression softened.

"Thanks."

The DJ changed the song to a slow ballad. Kids around us stopped talking and glommed onto each other like they were life rafts in the ocean. When I glanced up at Tyson, he had an expectant look. That was when I realized that his arms were outstretched.

"Dance with me?"

I chewed my lip. If we danced, people would know. It was possible that it would get back to Dad. But I didn't care. I wanted Tyson to hold me close, more than I wanted anything else in the world.

So I pushed out all my fears and nodded.

His arm slipped around my waist, and I lifted my hand and nestled it in his outstretched one. I wondered at how small mine looked next to his.

We just swayed back and forth, but I loved every minutes of it. It felt right. When he parted his lips, I shook my head.

"Please don't apologize for touching me. You promised."

He chuckled. It was quiet and surrounded me like a soft

blanket. "I wasn't going to apologize." His expression turned sheepish. "I guess I just felt selfish for touching you. And I didn't want to hurt you."

I met his gaze. "Hurt me? How could you hurt me?"

"Um." He glanced behind me as if he were fighting with what to say. "Because you're sweet and genuine. And I'm a mess."

"Well, you obviously have never seen me hungry." I raised my eyebrows.

"Oh really? That bad, huh?"

"Let's just say, those hangry commercials? I inspired those."

He nodded. "Good to know. Keep Tiny fed at all times. Got it."

I laughed. "That should be rule number one."

He shook his head. "Nope, can't be that. Rule number one is don't date Tiny." He leaned closer until he was inches from my ear. "But I'm kind of breaking that right now, aren't I?"

Warmth cascaded over me. Dating? Was that the rule he was breaking?

He pulled back and studied me, as if he were waiting to see my reaction. Not sure what to do, I just laughed.

"Yeah, my dad. He's crazy."

"I'm slowly understanding why he wanted to keep you protected." Tyson pulled me closer. "You're special."

I wrinkled my nose. "So we'll make 'keep Tiny fed at all

times' rule number two." I needed to change the subject before things got too serious.

He nodded. "Okay. Rule number two. I like it."

Before either of us could say anything, his phone rang. He dropped my hand and reached behind him to pull it from his back pocket. I glanced up, and his expression changed to one of worry.

"You okay?"

He shook his head. "I have to go. It's the babysitter. Cori's not feeling well."

I dropped my hands and nodded. "Yeah, okay. I understand."

He started to walk away but then paused. "You want to come?"

My eyes widened. "To your house?"

"Yeah."

Before I allowed myself to think it over, I nodded. "Of course."

CHAPTER THIRTEEN

IT TOOK the entire ride to Tyson's house for me to finally gather my wits about me. I still couldn't believe that I was alone with Tyson and that I was going to go into his house. I let out the breath I hadn't known I'd been holding as he pulled into his drive.

He glanced over at me and smiled. "Relax. Cori's going to love you."

I tried to laugh, but it came out more forced than anything. "I'm not nervous."

He raised his eyebrows. He didn't believe me—It was written all over his face.

So I nodded. "Okay, maybe a little."

He shot me another smile as he pulled his door handle and got out. I followed after him as he walked across his yard and up to the door. He headed inside, and I hesitated on the stoop. He glanced back at me.

"Come on, she won't bite."

I could hear cartoons playing in the background. A blue light glowed in the room to the left. I nodded and stepped inside.

Tyson slipped off his shoes and threw his keys in a bowl that sat on a small table in the corner.

"I'm here," he said as he made his way into the living room.

I bent down, slipping out of Rebecca's shoes and setting them next to Tyson's.

A squeal sounded from the other room, and a little girl with curly blonde hair jumped up from the couch. "Ty!" she screamed as she bounced a few times and jumped straight into his arms.

He pretended that she weighed a ton, bringing her close to the ground, then he pulled her back up and threw her into the air.

There was a moan from the couch as his mom's head appeared. "Keep her quiet, Tyson."

"When did Anna leave?" he asked. I could see the frustration written all over his face.

"Ten minutes ago."

He glanced down at Cori. "So, she's not sick, is she? You just texted me 'cause you don't want to deal with her. Didn't you."

"Don't Tyson," his mom snapped.

I saw his expression turn stony as he stared at her. Cori

was watching their interaction. Tyson must have noticed because he glanced down at her and smiled.

"This prince wants to put the princess to bed," he said as he leaned forward and gave her a kiss on the forehead.

My heart melted into a puddle of goo on the floor.

Cori squealed and Tyson wrapped her up in his arms and spun her around. That only made her laugh more.

"Tyson! Don't rile her up, or she'll never go to bed."

Tyson didn't seem to notice 'cause he stopped spinning and began throwing her up in the air. Cori laughed, throwing her head back.

Inwardly, I groaned. How was I ever going to stay away from him when he was rapidly becoming the best guy I'd ever known? I was supposed to be Switzerland here. Impartial. Seeing him only as my lab partner and study budy. I couldn't allow my heart to want more when, every time we got close, he just pulled away.

His mom must have shot him a murderous look, because he sighed, wrapped his arms around Cori, and motioned with his head for me to follow him. "I'll put her to bed," he called over his shoulder as we walked out of the room and I followed him up the stairs.

Cori must have noticed me as she peeked over his shoulder. "Who's that?" she asked, eyeing me.

I gave her a smile. For some reason, I really wanted her to like me.

"That's my friend."

She narrowed her eyes. "I've never seen her before. What's her name?"

When Tyson got to the top step, he turned and shifted her so she was on his arm. She laid her head on his shoulder, never breaking eye contact with me.

"Her name is Destiny. But I call her Tiny."

She grew quiet for a minute. "Is that like my name?"

"Yeah. Like your name. Corinne, but we call you Cori."

She wiggled, so he set her down. She walked up to me appraisingly. I never felt so nervous, standing there, being scrutinized by a kid that only came up to my bellybutton.

"Do you like princess movies?" she asked, folding her arms and tapping her foot on the floor.

"Of course. Who doesn't love princess movies?"

She narrowed her eyes. "What's your favorite?"

"Um..." I really wanted to say the right one. "The Frog Prince."

She grew quiet. Then turned her attention to Tyson. "I like her. She can stay."

Tyson laughed and stepped forward, scooping her up into his arms. A sense of relief washed over me. Was it weird that I was so happy that his little sister liked me?

"Come on, Tiny. I want to show you my room and my princess pajamas."

After she was dressed and her teeth brushed, she climbed into bed, patting the mattress next to her. "Can Tiny read me a story?"

Tyson glanced over at me. His eyes were wide. For a

moment, I sensed a glimpse of approval before he shrugged. "It's up to her. What do you say?"

"If that's okay. I don't want to step on anyone's toes," I said.

Tyson laughed as he walked over and grabbed a picture book from the bookshelf. "It's okay. I'm pretty tired of this one anyway. It needs new blood. Someone to breathe some life into the words."

He handed me a condensed version of Cinderella.

I nodded as I took it from him. Cori's eyes widened as if realizing I was actually going to read to her. She squealed and shifted over as I sat down.

I brought my feet up onto the bed, and she snuggled in next to me. My heart swelled for this little girl. I knew what it was like to have disappointing parents. But for me, I still had one that cared for me. She had none. Well, she had Tyson.

When I glanced over to where he had been standing, I saw the he'd moved over to a nearby chair. He was leaning forward with his elbows on his knees, watching me.

There was something so open and raw about his stare, that it made my heart pound in my chest. What was he thinking? It couldn't possibly be what I so desperately wanted it to be.

"You can start. I'm ready," Cori said as she yawned.

I snapped my gaze down to the book and nodded. "Of course." I flipped open the cover and started.

It was nice, sitting there with Cori, reading to her. As

much as I didn't want to admit it, it reminded me of when my mom used to read to me. And that made me sad. Made me long for a time when my life hadn't been so complicated. And having Tyson in the room made me both nervous and comfortable at the same time. I liked being in his presence, but it also scared me.

Just as I read the last sentence, Cori's chin dipped down onto her chest. Her breathing was slow and heavy, and she was no longer giggling at the way I read Gus Gus's voice.

"I think she's asleep."

I jumped. Tyson had left his spot on the chair and was now standing next to the bed. I took a deep breath, realizing how close he was to me.

Instead of focusing on the fact that he was standing over me, looking at me in a way that took my breath away, I turned to Cori and slowly shifted her off my shoulder and onto her pillow. After some Matrix-smooth moves, I was off the bed.

Tyson was inches from me, and it seemed he was not going to move. I needed to. I couldn't be this close to him.

I took a step forward, desperate to get away, when a sharp pain shot up my foot. I yelped and stumbled. Just as I placed my hands out, anticipating the fall, two hands wrapped around my waist and pulled me up.

"You okay?" Tyson asked. He kept his arms around me as he pulled me to his chest.

"Yep. Um hmm," I said, ignoring how good he smelled and how amazing it felt to be in his arms once more.

"Those Barbie shoes. They're dangerous."

I nodded as I wiggled my foot against the carpet, hoping to dull the lingering pain. It seemed to be working. Or maybe my body had just given up on transmitting the pain and had refocused its efforts on the feeling of Tyson pressed against me.

Good call, body. Good call.

"Come on, we should get out off here before she wakes up." He stepped away, sliding his hand down my arm and wrapping his fingers in mine.

My heart hammered so hard, I swear he could hear it. It was like all my emotions were rushing through my blood at a mile a second. I just hoped I didn't have a heart attack before this night was over.

Out in the hall, Tyson pulled Cori's door shut then hesitated. I watched him, wondering what he was thinking, hoping that he wouldn't pull away again.

"You did great in there," he said, bringing his gaze up to meet mine.

Oh, good, we were just going to chat. I could do that. Mindless talking. I smiled at him. "Thanks. She's a sweet girl. Almost makes me wish that I had a sibling." I pushed aside the pain that gripped my heart. Having a sibling would mean that Mom hadn't left, that I wouldn't have been abandoned.

He must have seen my face fall because he looked worried. "Are you okay?"

I chewed my lip and nodded. "Yeah. Just thinking about

my mom." My voiced dropped to a whisper. "And how she left. How everyone seems to leave." I didn't realize I had said those words until they lingered in the air. What was I doing? Why was I saying these things to him? He had enough problems in his life to worry about. My sad childhood shouldn't be one of them.

He stepped closer to me, meeting my gaze. My heart picked up speed. "She's an idiot."

I cleared my throat. What was happening? "Who?" I asked.

He focused on me. "Your mom. Only an idiot would leave you." He reached out, grabbed my hand, and pulled me closer to him.

And I knew. I knew he was going to kiss me, and that was all I wanted him to do. He reached out his other hand to cradle my cheek and then dipped down to press his lips against mine.

It was gentle at first. Like he was seeing how I would react. This time, I didn't hesitate. I dropped his hand and wrapped my fingers together at the base of his neck, pulling him closer to me to deepen the kiss. I wanted him to know how I felt.

He took control, moving me back until I was pressed against the wall. He lifted me up so I was level with him, using the wall to support me. I tangled my hands into his hair and let him kiss me.

Every moment. Every heart-breaking moment we'd

shared earlier today was washed away. All I cared about was Tyson and me. That was it.

Moments later, he pulled away and set me down on the ground. His breath was deep, and his gaze held an intensity that weakened my knees. I was thankful for the support the wall gave me.

He pressed his hands on either side of me as if he too needed that support. After a few deep breaths, he met my gaze again. And I saw it. Worry. Regret. All the things that I wanted to beg him not to feel. This was *right*. I liked him, and I was pretty convinced that he liked me too.

"Tiny, I..." His voice was deep as if emotion was choking his throat. When he glanced up at me, I could see the conflict in his gaze.

"It's okay," I said, even though my heart broke from those two little words. It wasn't okay. I wanted to be with him. And he wanted to be with me. And even if I said I understood why he felt we couldn't be together, the truth was, I didn't.

He shook his head. "I like you, Tiny. You're different. And I like that. But—"

I pressed my finger to his lips. I couldn't hear those words again. I wanted to bask in the moment for a bit longer before reality crashed down around us.

He raised his eyebrows but didn't say anything more. Instead, we just stood there, inches from each other. We didn't say anything. We just lived in this moment. Lived in what it meant. And what it could never be.

He reached up and cradled my cheek. He brushed his thumb against my lips, sending shivers across my skin.

How was I ever going to be the same after this? There are defining moments in everyone's life, and the moments that I'd shared with Tyson carried that weight. I wasn't going to be able to walk away unscathed. He'd changed me. I just wished I could tell him.

I wished that he wanted to hear how I felt. But he looked so broken as it was. I didn't want to burden him with my problems as well.

I reached up, wrapped my arms around him, and pulled him close. He was a friend, and I wanted to show him that. He responded by wrapping his arms around my waist and holding me tight.

We stood there, in his hallway, outside of his little sister's door, holding each other. If his phone hadn't started ringing, we could have stayed there forever.

But he broke our hug and pulled out his phone, glancing down at it.

"Huh, that party we were at? Apparently it got broken up by the cops. Crazy, right?" I saw him smile as the phone lit up his face.

"Yeah." And then I realized that I never told Rebecca I was leaving with Tyson. She was probably worried about me. "My phone," I said, stepping toward the staircase.

"You okay?" Tyson asked, following after me.

"I forgot to tell Rebecca that I went with you. She's probably freaking out." I padded down the stairs and over to my purse, which I'd left by my shoes. I grabbed it and pulled out my phone.

I'd been right. There were at least fifteen texts from her. I clicked on the last one, and my heart sank.

Rebecca: Tiny, I hope you don't hate me, but I can't find you. I had to call your dad to see if you were home. Please, don't be mad at me. I'm just so worried.

My stomach flipped as I swallowed. I needed to get home. Right now.

I glanced up, and Tyson must have seen my worried expression because his eyebrows were drawn together.

"What happened?" he asked.

"You need to take me home. Now."

CHAPTER FOURTEEN

TYSON TURNED DOWN MY STREET, and I held up my hand.

"Drop me off here," I said.

He nodded and pulled over. I unbuckled my seatbelt and let it slide back. I wanted to leave and stay at the same time. I had a pretty good idea about how Dad was going to react, and I really didn't want to face him right now. Plus, I knew the moment I got out of the car, the magic of this evening would evaporate like rain on a hot summer day.

"I'm sorry if I got you in trouble," Tyson said. I felt his gaze on me.

I turned and shrugged. "It's no biggie. Dad will get over it." Truth was, I didn't know if that was true. I'd never done something so grievous that he had to "get over it." If his inability to move past what Mom did was any indication, then I had no chance of saying anything that would calm him down. Or instill his trust in me again.

"Well, if he grounds you forever, I promise to come visit you." There was a playful hint to his voice.

I glanced over at him. "I'll hold you to that. You might have to slay a dragon to get to me, but I expect that you'd chance bodily harm to see me again."

He did a mini bow in his seat. "Yes, m'lady."

I grabbed my purse and pulled on the handle. "I'll see you later."

Tyson's expression grew serious. "I hope so."

I hated it when he did that. When he made me hope. I was pretty sure that it was just his flirty side coming out. He wasn't intentionally hurting me over and over again. But it did. Every time.

He dropped his smile as if he suddenly realized what he'd said. "Sorry, Tiny. I didn't mean to—"

I shrugged. "It's fine. It's really a fact more than anything else. You will see me on Monday. So..." I shrugged and stepped out onto the curb.

Just then, a yellow Bug drove by. But I ducked down next to his car out of instinct. Once it was gone, I straightened, smoothing out my skirt and shooting him a sheepish look.

"Maybe you should text me tonight. Just so I know that your dad didn't kill you or anything."

I snorted. "I think you'd be the one he'd come after if anything."

His skin paled, and I waved away his worry. "I'm not going to tell him. I want us to go to state as well, and dropping his best player would be stupid."

He wiped at his brow. "Whew. Thanks."

Before our conversation went down the path that only led to heartbreak for me, I gave him a thumbs up, stepped away from the car, and shut the door.

I watched as he drove away and then started the long and anxiety-inducing walk to my house. When I got to the front walkway, I glanced up at the windows.

Every light was on.

My stomach squeezed. This wasn't good.

I took a deep breath and made my way to the front door. After I pushed the door open, I paused, listening.

"I just don't understand why she would lie to me like that," Dad's voice carried from the living room.

My brow furrowed. Who was he talking to?

"She's a teenage girl. I'm sure it's not unheard of."

Was that Ms. Swallow? What was she doing here?

I stepped into the entryway and dropped my purse down on the table. "I'm here."

I heard scrambling and then Dad appeared.

"Where have you been?" He folded his arms and narrowed his eyes.

Go with an apology. "I'm so sorry, Dad. I didn't mean for things to get out of hand."

"You said there weren't going to be boys there, and then

I get a call from Rebecca telling me she can't find you." His face reddened from just saying the words.

My thoughts flashed back to the kiss Tyson and I shared and then the image of Dad's head exploding if he ever found out.

"I realized that the party was getting out of hand, so I left. I forgot to call Bec, and my phone was on silent." I cringed as the lies kept piling up. But it wasn't only me that would be affected by Dad finding out about me and Tyson. It could hurt Tyson as well. So I pushed forward. "I decided to walk, which is why I'm home now."

"Sounds like a responsible move." Ms. Swallow appeared behind Dad. She gave me an encouraging smile.

"Hey," I said, nodding at her and then I glanced between the two of them. "What is Ms. Swallow doing here?"

Dad lifted his finger. "Don't change the subject. I am not the one on trial here. You were out, with boys, and you lied to me." He sighed. "I'm disappointed, Tiny."

Ms. Swallow reached out and rested her hand on his forearm. "But she left when she realized that the party was getting out of hand. You have to admit, that shows some good integrity."

I tried not to grimace. Why was Ms. Swallow still talking? It was like she was heaping the guilt on me. I really wanted her to stop.

"I'm really tired. I just want to go to sleep. We can talk

about this in the morning." I ducked my head and began to walk past them.

Dad grunted, but didn't say anything more. I wondered if Ms. Swallow had hinted that he should let me go.

Once I moved past them, I glanced into the living room, where the TV was on and there were two glasses of wine and a bowl of popcorn sitting on the coffee table.

Were they on a date? A sour feeling took up residence in my gut. Ugh. What was happening? How could Dad be so upset about me spending time with the opposite sex when he was doing the same thing? It felt hypocritical and made me angry.

But I wasn't going to push my luck right now. I was going to head upstairs, take a shower, text Rebecca that I was safe, and then go to bed. In the morning, I'd face all my feelings about Ms. Swallow and Dad. And maybe, my feelings about Tyson.

DAD WAS in the kitchen when I came downstairs the next morning. He was sitting at the table, drinking a mug of coffee. Steam rose from the dark liquid in white wisps.

I nodded to him as I passed by on my way over to the cupboard, where I grabbed a glass and filled it with water. I could feel his gaze on me. I wasn't sure what I wanted to say to him, so I poured myself some cereal and leaned against the counter.

"I wanted to apologize for getting so upset last night."

I was grateful that he'd decided to be the one to break the silence. I was mid-bite, so I just nodded. Once I'd swallowed, I said, "I'm sorry I misled you. It wasn't my intention."

He folded up the newspaper that was spread across the table. "I know you would never intentionally deceive me."

That statement was like a kick to my gut. Ugh. Why did he have to say that? I felt like a terrible person and an even worse daughter. But I wanted to be able to see Tyson—even though it hurt—and owning up to everything didn't seem like the smart move to make.

So I shrugged, drank the remaining milk in my bowl, and rinsed it out. "I love you, Dad." At least that wasn't another lie.

"I know, Tiny. I love you, too." He stood and walked over.

When he wrapped me in a hug, the guilt dug deeper into my chest. How had everything become so complicated? Why was me liking a guy so terrible to him? If he just got to know Tyson, then I knew he'd like him too. After all, Tyson was so responsible that he acted like he had the world on his shoulders, and Dad could relate to that.

Maybe that was the solution. If I could just get Tyson and Dad to talk, maybe Dad would realize that Tyson was a good guy and let go of his ridiculous expectation that I die a nun.

It could work.

I gave him a good squeeze, and we broke apart. Dad rinsed out his coffee cup, and I waited around the kitchen. It was Saturday. The day we normally did something, just the two of us.

Dad set his mug down in the sink and then turned. "What do you want to do today?"

I threaded my fingers and cracked my knuckles. "Oh, I was thinking about kicking your butt at mini golf."

He raised his eyebrows. "I feel a challenge coming on."

I laughed. "Oh, old man, you don't want to challenge me."

"Them are fighting words. You sure you want to go head-to-head with your *old man?*"

I pretended to punch his bicep. "Oh yeah."

He laughed and nodded. "Alrighty, Pirate's Cove it is. But don't go crying if I beat you."

"Ha! You always say that and yet never do." I raised my hands as if I were addressing my adoring fans. "I *am* reigning champion."

Dad scoffed. "Well, be prepared to be taken down." He leaned in and narrowed his eyes. "It's time."

"Thirty minutes. I need to shower and get dressed." I skipped toward the stairs.

"Sounds good," Dad said as he smiled over at me. "Hey, Tiny?" he called right before I disappeared.

I hesitated and turned. "Yeah?"

"Make sure to bring a bucket for all your tears."

I laughed a maniacal laugh and then took the stairs two

at a time. Once I was showered, I dressed in a pair of shorts and a flowy t-shirt and made my way downstairs to find Dad sitting on the couch, studying his phone.

He leaned over it and typed with his thumbs. Like he was texting someone. But who? I didn't think that Dad even texted his friends.

"Xavier?" I asked as I grabbed my Converses from the entryway and walked over to the couch.

Dad snapped his gaze up, dropping his phone to his leg. "What?"

I stared at him. Wow, he was acting strange. "Are you texting Xavier?" Then I shook my head. "Wait, that wasn't what I wanted to ask. What I meant was, since when do you text your friends?"

"I'm not that old. My friends and I text."

I snorted as I slipped my feet into my shoes. "Right."

When my gaze made its way over to the coffee table, I saw the wine glasses from the night before.

Ms. Swallow.

How on earth could I have forgotten?

"So, that was weird, huh? Ms. Swallow being here last night." I eyed him, waiting to see his response.

Just as I suspected, his cheeks flushed pink. "Yeah, it was nice of her to come hang out with an old fart like me."

Hang out? Old fart? What was with him? He never talked like that and most definitely didn't act all flustered when talking about another teacher.

"Was it a date?"

"A date? What? No."

There that voice was again. Something was going on and he was not being truthful about it. "Isn't there some rule in every parenting book that says you shouldn't introduce your children to your girlfriend until you're sure it's serious?"

My chest squeezed. Why was I reacting this way? What did it matter if he liked Ms. Swallow? I didn't care. Except, he'd forbidden me to fall in love, and I felt a bit betrayed that he seemed just fine with it happening to him.

"Ms. Swallow is not my girlfriend." He sighed and leaned back. "And if she were, there's not a lot I can do about you not meeting her. She is your teacher."

I stood, suddenly feeling really anxious. "Ugh, Dad. Why would you even entertain the idea of you and her? What happened to 'love sucks'? You always say that boys leave you brokenhearted and pregnant."

Dad laughed, making me more upset. I hated that he thought I was being funny. "Angelica is not a hormonal teenage boy. I figured I didn't have to make that clear."

I rolled my eyes. "Because every boy is just out to take my flower..." Back track. This was not a conversation I wanted to have with my dad. "I mean, virtue."

Dad's face turned bright red. How had this conversation gone so horribly? I swallowed and tried to still my frustration.

"It just feels a little hypocritical that you're here, unsupervised with a member of the opposite sex, and yet I can't go to a fully staffed party with some boys." I folded my arms.

A stony expression passed over his face. He stood, tucked his phone into his pocket and then folded his arms. "The difference is, I am an adult. You are a child. While you are under my roof, you will follow my rules. I don't have to explain myself or my actions."

He walked over to the front door and opened it. "Now, are you ready to play?"

I stared at him. This was not cool in so many ways. Dad had never acted like this before. And maybe it was because I was rebelling. But I was beginning to realize that maybe it wasn't me. Maybe it was him. And right now, he was the one that needed to change.

So I slipped my shoes off and shook my head. "I'm not in the mood anymore," I said as I turned and headed back up to my room.

CHAPTER FIFTEEN

I DIDN'T FEEL any better an hour later. Sulking in my room did nothing for my mood. I felt bad. I hadn't meant to snap at Dad like that. I was frustrated. Not only was Dad in my head, but the cute guy at school who liked me was using Dad's stupid rule as a reason to stay away from me.

It wasn't fair.

As frustration rose up in my chest, I groaned and rolled off the bed. I needed to get out of the house before I drove myself insane. I made my way over to my desk and picked up my phone that was still charging from last night.

I had a text from Rebecca, singing hallelujah that I was still alive. And then another one cursing me for leaving her and not letting her know where I was going.

And then there was one from Tyson. My heart picked up speed as I pressed on it with my thumb.

Tyson: I'm hoping that you've gone to bed

and you not texting me is not because your dad killed you for coming home late.

I laughed, heat racing to my cheeks. I liked him. I really liked him. And even though he kept saying we could never be anything, I was drawn to him.

Maybe I should see a therapist about that. Constantly doing the same thing but expecting a different result was the definition of insanity.

I sighed as I flopped down on my bed.

Me: Nope. Not dead. Sorry to disappoint.

I laid the phone next to me and closed my eyes. Talking to Tyson had a healing effect on me. Suddenly, I didn't care about Dad or how disappointed he would be if he found out I was talking to Tyson. He had his secrets—I could have mine.

Tyson: Why would I be disappointed that you are alive? Now I can tell Cori to stop bugging me about texting you.

I laughed. Cori was talking about me? I liked that his little sister liked me. Maybe she could convince him that I should become a more permanent fixture in his life.

Me: Aww, tell Cori I miss her too.

The next text came faster this time.

Tyson: Bad idea. Now she wants to see you again. Apparently, I look terrible in a gown and heels. She wants someone who looks like a princess, and I'm not making the cut.

Me: This I have to see. You in heels? Genius!

Tyson: I don't think I'd ever come back from that.

I waited for him to text me more. It felt strange that he just left the conversation like that.

Tyson: Sorry. Squirt is bugging me again. So, what do you say? Help a guy out? Appease his little sister?

My heart began to race. Tyson wanted to see me again? After last night, I figured it would take a miracle for us to get together again. Well, a miracle or chemistry.

Me: Sure. What did you have in mind?

Tyson: The screams that come out of that girl. I think she woke up every dog in the neighborhood and they are all now howling. You're making a little girl very happy. How about I come grab you in a half hour?

Me: Perfect

Luckily, by the time I made my way downstairs, Dad was gone. He left a note about needing to run some errands. He apologized for what happened and said if I was going anywhere, to make sure I leave a note.

So I did just that. I left a note saying I was going out. I didn't tell him where I was going or who I was going with. Just that I was gone.

Tyson pulled up in front of my house with an apologetic look on his face. I smiled as I opened the door and climbed in. Cori was basically jumping up and down on her booster seat. Thankfully, she had a seatbelt on.

"You ready?" he asked.

I nodded as I pulled the seatbelt over my lap. "So, where are we going?" I asked, turning to give Cori a huge grin.

"I wanna tell her. I wanna tell her," Cori yelled.

Tyson laughed. "Okay, squirt. You can tell her."

"Princess land!" She screamed, pumping her fists in the air.

"Princess land?" I asked, turning to see Tyson grinning as he studied the road.

"That's what she calls Disneyland."

I laughed as I settled back in my seat. "It's the perfect place for a little girl."

Twenty minutes later, we pulled up to the parking lot. After Tyson paid, he found a spot and turned off the car. Cori was already out of her seat and pulling on the door handle.

"Cori," Tyson said, his voice growing serious.

I could see the frustration in her face when she turned around. She knew his tone and what it meant.

"You need to wait until one of us is out. I don't want you getting hit by a car," he said.

She sighed and nodded.

After I got out, I opened her door, and she hopped out. "Thanks, Tiny," she said, smiling up at me and threading her hand through mine.

I stared at our clasped hands. Was it wrong that I loved

the fact that she liked me? Maybe it'd help Tyson realize that we were perfect for each other. After all, didn't kids have like a sixth sense? They could tell if someone was bad or good. If Cori liked me, I was obviously good.

Tyson rounded the car and glanced down at our clasped hands and then up to meet my gaze. He had a softness to his countenance. I wanted to read into it. I wanted to tell myself it was because he cared about me. But I'd put myself out there so many times now, and he just rejected me, time and time again.

I didn't think I could handle another round of *I can't do this, please forget what I just did.* Right now, with everything going on with Dad, I didn't think I could handle another hit. I'd shatter for sure.

At the gate, Tyson stepped up to the ticket agent. She looked him over and told him the amount for the three of us. But there was no way I was going to let him pay for me. He was strapped for cash.

"Just for the two. I'm paying for myself."

Tyson glanced over at me. "I don't think so, Tiny. I'm paying for you as well." He pulled out his card and set it down on the counter.

I stared at him. "No. I'll pay for myself." I reached into my purse and pulled out some cash.

Just as I laid it down, his hand rested on mine. My heart picked up speed from the contact. I swallowed, hating myself for the reaction I got from a simple gesture. I didn't want to have feelings for him, but I couldn't help it. I did.

"Please, let me pay." There was an earnest look in his eyes that told me to slide my hand out from under his and stuff my money back into my purse.

I nodded, the woman ran his card, and we were walking into the park a few minutes later. Within steps of the entrance, a man with a camera around his neck stepped up to us.

"A picture for the memory?" he asked.

Tyson glanced over at me. "Um, sure."

He positioned us out of the sun with Cori between Tyson and me. After a few seconds, he shook his head and lowered his camera.

"Can you two stand closer together?" he asked, waving his hand between us.

I glanced over at Tyson, who hesitated and then nodded. It was like he was moving in slow motion. He stuck his arm out, wrapped it around my waist, and pulled me close. My breath caught in my throat as I reveled in the feeling of his body pressed against mine. Suddenly, we were outside of Cori's room again and he was pressing me against the wall, kissing me.

I wanted to feel that again.

He finished taking the picture, handed us a ticket, and told us we could pick it up at the nearby kiosk anytime during our stay here. Tyson pocketed the paper and then turned to Cori.

For a brief moment, I saw him brush his thumb against his fingertips. As if he were trying to rub away a feeling. Did he have the same reaction from our touch as I did? If that was the truth, why couldn't he be honest with me?

Cori was already bounding away, so I didn't have time to stand there and examine his intentions, instead, I followed after them.

"Where're you going, Cori?" he asked, quickening his pace to follow after her.

"To meet the princesses," she called over her shoulder.

When we finally caught up with her, Tyson grabbed her around the waist and hoisted her up onto his shoulders. We walked in silence for a few seconds. I couldn't help but notice how close his arm was to mine. It would be so natural to reach out and entwine my fingers with his.

"Thanks," he said, breaking the silence.

I glanced over. "For what?"

He smiled his million-watt smile, and I melted just a bit. "For coming with me. It's great that we can still be friends."

My heart stopped. *Friends.* He wanted to be friends. I swallowed, forcing down my feelings of defeat as I glanced up at him. "Of course. We will always be friends. Besides, I'm here for Cori." Then I leaned closer to him. "Besides, my princess tank was running dangerously low, so really, you're doing me a favor."

He laughed, and I tried not to stare at the way his eyes crinkled at the corners. "Well, if that's the case, then you're welcome."

"Churro!" Cori screamed, pulling Tyson's head toward the man in a costume selling churros.

"Jeez, Cori. You don't have to pull on me."

Before he could resist, I pulled out my wallet and walked over. After paying for two extremely overpriced cinnamon-sugared churros, I handed one to Cori and offered half of the other to Tyson. He took it, but not before giving me a pointed look.

I shrugged as I broke off a piece and put it in my mouth. "What?" I asked.

He kept his gaze on me as he took a bite. "You need to stop doing that. This is my treat. That means I pay."

I rolled my eyes. "Why? We're *friends*. That means I pay for myself."

A pained expression passed over his face. It was nice to see that he liked that word as much as I did. I wasn't the only crazy person in this relationship.

"You're not going to make this easy on me, are you Tiny?"

I gave him a mischievous look and shook my head. "Yeah, no."

Before he could respond, he brushed his hand through his hair. "Hey, squirt. Getting any cinnamon sugar in your mouth?"

Cori giggled and took another bite. "We're almost there!" she squealed, bouncing up and down and pointing to the building that looked as if it came straight from the movie *Beauty and the Beast*. Scrawled across the front was the words "Royal Hall: Greet the Princesses."

It was probably out of necessity, but Tyson swung Cori

down and set her on the ground. She cheered as she approached the doors. And then stopped.

Tyson glanced over at me with his eyebrows raised. I shrugged. We approached her to find that she had wide eyes and a downturned mouth.

"What's the matter, Cor?" Tyson asked, wrapping his arm around her shoulders.

She glanced over at him. "I'm not a princess," she said, pulling at her shirt.

My heart melted. "Yes you are," I said, kneeling down next to her.

She looked at me, and I saw that she had tears welling up in her eyes. "No. My dad said he would get me a princess dress for my birthday, but..." Her voice drifted off as a huge tear rolled down her cheek.

Tyson scooped her up and walked over to the center of the courtyard, where he set her down right underneath the Rapunzel statue. He knelt down in front of her. Cori had her face covered with her hands by now. She was sobbing into them, her shoulders shaking.

"Hey, princess, hey," Tyson said, pulling at her hands.

Cori fought it for a moment before she let him move them away. He reached out and wiped away the tears with his thumb.

"Cori, it's okay," he said, dipping down to meet her gaze.

She sniffled and nodded, her body shaking from the movement.

"Even though your dad's gone, I'm here. I'll take care

of you," he said, reaching out and wrapping his arms around her. "You're my girl." His voice was muffled from her hair.

She pulled back and placed both hands on his cheeks. "You're my Prince Charming," she said, staring into his eyes.

He nodded. "I want to be."

She hesitated and then nodded. "Yes." She flung her arms around his neck. He straightened and spun her around. After a few seconds, she squealed as she flung her head back.

When he stopped and set her on the ground, she looked up at him expectantly. He shrugged. "What?"

"Now it's Tiny's turn," she said, waving in my direction.

I glanced down at her. "What? My turn for what?"

She smiled up at me. "Tell her that she's a princess and you are her Prince Charming."

My eyes widened. That was the last thing I wanted to hear. "Oh, sweetie, that's okay. I'm good." I swallowed, hoping my rejection of her offer would work.

But I should have known. Instead of understanding, she shook her head, grabbed my hand, and shoved it into Tyson's. "Nope. Every princess needs a Prince Charming." She leaned closer to me. "I'll loan you mine."

I nodded, hopefully the movement wasn't as dorky as it felt. "That's generous of you."

After my hand was firmly gripped by Tyson, Cori stepped back to watch. She waved for him to continue. I could feel his presence as he moved closer to me. It was one of those instances where we weren't touching, but I was distinctly aware of his proximity to me.

"You don't have to—"

He shook his head. "She won't let this go." He glanced down at me, and I could see a smile playing on his lips.

Why was he so confident? I hated that, in an instant, he could turn me into a bumbling fool. And yet he remained as relaxed as could be.

He steadied his gaze. "Tiny, you are—"

"Touch her cheek, like you did with me," Cori interjected.

He glanced over at her and raised his eyebrows. From the corner of my eye, I saw her no-nonsense expression. I chuckled. "You're in trouble when she's a teenager."

He winced. "Don't say those words. She's going to be a nun."

Before I could respond, he reached up and cradled my cheek with his hand. There was a familiarity to his touch that caused my heart to swell. He was becoming a part of me. I knew him.

He glanced down at me, and his gaze turned serious. "Tiny, you are a princess and I"—I watched him swallow, his Adam's apple rising and falling—"am your Prince Charming." His last words lingered on his lips. My gaze dipped down to study them.

For a moment, it seemed as if he were leaning closer. Like I'd seen him do twice before. And I wanted him to. I wanted—no needed—him to kiss me.

"Yeah!" Cori screamed, breaking the connection between us. She wrapped both arms around us and jumped up and down. "Now, let's go get pretty." She reached up and grabbed my hand, pulling me toward the Bippity Bobbity Boutique, where we disappeared inside.

The last glimpse I had of Tyson, he had a contemplative expression on his face as he stood under the Rapunzel statue, watching us go.

CHAPTER SIXTEEN

AFTER ENOUGH HAIRSPRAY and bobby pins to last me a lifetime, Cori and I emerged from the boutique covered in glitter and taffeta. Thankfully—and much to Cori's dismay—they did not have princess costumes for adults. Apparently, it was frowned upon.

After her mini tantrum in the store, we picked out her Belle costume, and that seemed to appease her. I couldn't talk her out of my getting a makeover, however. That was one persistent girl.

I paid, and we headed off to find Tyson. He was sitting next to Maurice's Treats eating a bagel-twisty thing. When he saw us, his eyes widened. He stood and cleared his throat as he dumped the rest of his food into the nearby garbage.

"What happened to Cori? All I see is Belle." He searched around, looking for her.

She giggled and pulled on his hand. "I'm right here, Ty."

He continued to search for a few more seconds before he glanced at her. "Oh, there you are." He bent down, scooped her up, and planted a kiss on her forehead.

I watched, secretly hoping Cori would insist that he do the same to me. Then my stomach flipped, and I pushed that thought from my mind.

"They didn't have dresses for Tiny," she said, pushing out her bottom lip.

His gaze made its way over to me, and he smiled. "But I see they did your makeup."

I tugged at the curls that framed my face. "Yeah. Your sister is very persistent."

He laughed. "That's one way to classify her." He pulled Cori close and looked her in the eye. "Wanna go meet the princesses now?"

She nodded. "Yes."

We walked over to the entrance of the Royal Hall and waited while a man in a purple costume, complete with a feathered hat, held up his hand. The sign out front read, 15 minute wait. I stood by, listening to Cori recount every detail of the boutique to Tyson.

He nodded and smiled. I could tell he wasn't that interested in what she was saying, but he was a good brother. He cared about her so much that it made my heart hurt.

I felt bad for how I'd treated Dad. Sure, he could be a dork and didn't handle situations the best, but he was my dad. The only family I had. And if there was one thing

Tyson had taught me, family was everything. It was our responsibility to protect each other no matter what.

I must have been staring at him because he raised his eyebrows. "Do I have something on my face?"

I blinked a few times and then shook my head. Heat rose to my cheeks. "No, sorry."

He chuckled as the costumed man waved us in. We rounded a wood divider and Cori squealed as Cinderella came into view. The princess dipped down and wrapped her arms around Cori, who stood there with her eyes wide, listening to Cinderella's questions.

"You just helped me realize how important family is," I said, leaning closer to Tyson. He smelled so good. Like the woods after it rained.

"I did?"

"Yeah. Dad and I fought earlier. Apparently, he's upset that there were guys at the party last night. I told him he could trust me, but you know how he is."

Tyson winced and nodded. "Yeah. He's a little extreme."

Cori took a picture with Cinderella and then took off around the corner. We chased her down just to find her hugging Sleeping Beauty.

Tyson was quiet, so I glanced over at him. He was watching Cori with a contemplative look. My stomach squeezed. I didn't like his expression, and I was pretty sure I knew what he was thinking about.

"Hey, Tiny," he said, leaning toward me.

I cleared my throat. I wanted to tell him to be quiet. To not say the words that I could see were on the tip of his tongue.

"I think you and I should take a break. It's not right, us sneaking around like this." He swallowed as he kept his gaze on Cori. I wondered if he was being a responsible brother or if he just couldn't meet my gaze.

I hoped it was the first one. "What?" I asked, the lump had swollen in my throat, making it hard to speak.

He toed the maroon carpet with his shoe. "If some guy asked Cori to lie and sneak around behind my back, well..." He let his voice trail off as his jaw clenched.

I bit down the emotions that were rising up in my chest. How could I convince him not to finish that thought? "But it's ridiculous. The rule is stupid. He can't control my life like that." I wanted Tyson to stop talking. I wanted him to wrap his arms around me and tell me to stay forever. But those words were not coming. I blinked, hoping to keep the tears from welling up.

Too late.

"Tiny, it's for the best. And what if we continued? How would we explain this?" He rubbed his hand through his hair. "I can't lose my scholarship. And if he kicks me off the team, it's gone." He cleared his throat. "I can't do that to Cori. I'm her only hope of getting out of the mess that is my mom's house."

I watched as she gleefully took a picture with Sleeping Beauty then took off again. We followed her, this time with much less vigor. I knew what he was saying was true. There was no way Dad would just let this go. He'd punish me and he'd punish Tyson. And for Tyson, it would be much worse.

So we needed to part ways—before everything fell down around us. For Tyson sake, and Cori's.

We spent the rest of our time at Disneyland faking happiness for Cori. She grinned at each princess she got to meet, and she loved the *Beauty and the Beast* play at the theatre across from the Royal Hall.

Tyson was a much better faker than me because, numerous times, Cori asked me what was wrong. I forced a smile and told her "nothing," I was happy I was there. Which I was, I just dreaded what was going to happen when we left. We'd be over.

Cori. Tyson. They would leave this gaping, gushing, bleeding hole in my heart. And there was no way I could stop it. It was Mom all over again. Leaving me. Abandoning me.

Despite my desperate plea to the powers that be for the day to slow down, Tyson picked up a very tired Cori and waved toward the exit. "We should get this princess home before she turns into a pumpkin."

I nodded and followed after them, carrying her wand and shoes. By the time we got to the car, she'd fallen asleep. Tyson buckled her into her seat and shut her door. I lingered next to the car, not wanting to get in. Was it wrong that I didn't want this night to end?

"You okay?" he asked, eyeing me.

I chewed my lip, keeping my emotions in check. "Yeah. I'll be okay."

His expression wavered as he began to nod. "Good. I'm glad you're on board."

He pulled open the driver's door and climbed in.

I sucked in my breath and blew out every painful emotion that had built up in my chest. I could do this. Couldn't I?

It took the whole ride home to discover that I most certainly could not do this. I couldn't be just friends again. If we were going to end our relationship, I was going to have to cut all ties. Everything.

"I'll let Ms. Swallow know she should find you a new partner," I said as I ran my finger along the window control button.

Tyson glanced over at me. "You don't have to do that."

I pinched my lips together and nodded. "Yes, I do. I can't do both. Be around you and not be with you." I hesitated as I waited to hear what he was going to say. Would he understand what I was trying to tell him?

But he just nodded his head. "Okay. Yeah, that's probably a good idea."

Knife to the chest. That was not what I wanted to hear. Tyson Blake didn't care for me like I cared for him. It was going to be over, and in the end, I was the one standing there with a broken heart.

"Glad you're on board," I said, sarcasm dripping from my words. I wanted to say so much more. Dad was right.

The opposite sex was only designed to play with your emotions and then rip your heart out.

As soon as he pulled into my driveway, I opened the door and hopped out. He started to say something, but I slammed the door on his words. I didn't want to hear what he had to say. Whatever noble reason he had for why we couldn't be together was the last thing I wanted to have occupying my thoughts.

I wanted to hate him right now. I needed to hate him. If not, I was never going to get through this breakup. I needed to believe that he was a jerk.

Because deep down, I knew that was a lie.

I shoved all my feelings for him away and opened the front door. I needed to get my head on straight because, in a few seconds, I'd need to account for the entire day. I knew Dad was not going to be happy if I didn't tell him what I'd been up to. Preparation was key to keeping Dad in the dark.

The screen door slammed behind me as I walked into the entryway.

"Dad," I called out. "I'm home."

No rage machine came from around the corner. In fact, it was creepily quiet. I glanced around. It was past seven. Where was he?

"Hello?"

A muffled voice carried from the kitchen. I rounded the corner to see Ms. Swallow standing next to the counter with her phone up to her ear.

". . .well, if you hear from her, will you please have her

call me?" She hesitated before she nodded. "Yes, that's my number."

"Why are you here?" I asked.

She turned and her eyes widened. She thanked the other person on the phone and then set it down next to her. "Where have you been?" she asked, stepping toward me.

I stared at her. Why was she asking where I'd been? It wasn't like she was my mom or anything. I barely even knew the woman. "Where's my dad?" I asked, glancing behind her.

When she didn't answer, I looked back. There was a look in her eye that told me something was wrong.

"Ms. Swallow?"

She took a deep breath. "He's in the ICU. He was in a car accident." She wrung her hands together. She was shaking.

My ears were ringing as I stumbled to a chair by the table and sat down. "He's what?"

"We were out this afternoon, and he dropped me off at the door and went to park. There was no parking in the lot, so he went to the road. He was hit by a car that was going too fast as he crossed the street." Her breathing became shallow as she pinched her eyes shut. "I watched the whole thing."

I wanted to vomit. I wanted her to stop talking. My legs, arms, and face felt numb. "Is he going to be okay?" I hesitated. Did I want to know?

"Yes. He should be fine. He broke his leg and has a

major concussion, but the doctors are confident that he will make a full recovery."

I stood up, anger coursing through my veins. I was mad at so many things, and right now, most of them boiled down to Ms. Swallow. It was her fault that I had gotten to know Tyson. It was her fault that Dad had been out today and got hurt. And it was her fault that I'd gotten so freaked out, for not telling me right away that he was going to be okay.

"Next time, lead with that," I said, standing up and heading toward the side door.

"Where are you going?" she called after me.

I shot her an annoyed look. "To see my dad." I pulled the door open and glanced toward the place Dad normally parked. Nothing.

"The car's still at the restaurant. I can take you over there if you want."

"Haven't you done enough?" The words spilled from my lips before I could stop them.

I saw her wince, and for a moment, I felt bad. Logically, I knew it wasn't her fault. But I needed someone to blame. She was here, so she was the cause.

I raised my eyebrows. "I guess you can take me if I have no other choice." I reached up to tuck my hair behind my ear and felt the crunchiness of the hairspray from my makeover. Crap. I couldn't go see Dad like this. "Let me wash my face real quick," I said, slipping up the back stairs. "Bec and I did makeovers," I called down to her.

I didn't need her spilling to Dad who I'd been with.

When I got to my room, I washed my face and pulled my hair up into a messy bun. Five minutes later, I was back downstairs, where Ms. Swallow was leaning against the kitchen counter.

I shot her a look as I passed by. "Come on," I said, waving toward the darkening sky.

"Hang on," she said, holding up a finger.

I stared at her. Why was she doing this? I wanted to see my dad, not stand there and talk to her.

"You said you were with Rebecca?"

I nodded. "Yeah."

She tapped her chin. "That's interesting, because when I was trying to track you down, I called Rebecca and she said she had no idea where you were."

I swallowed. "Well, did you try to call my phone?"

"Yes. It went straight to your voicemail."

I pulled out my phone, and the screen stayed black. Somehow, I'd forgotten to charge it last night. It was dead. I sighed and shoved it back into my purse. "Well, I decided to go to the library to study. They had a face painter there." I swallowed. This lie was getting worse and worse.

Ms. Swallow sighed as she unfolded her arms. "Listen, Destiny. I know you're upset." She took a step toward me and smiled. "I want you to know that I'm here. You can talk to me if you want. We can be friends."

There that word was again. Friends.

How could I be friends with someone who was not only my teacher but was seeing my dad? And I wasn't even going to start on how weird it was to think both of those things in one sentence.

So I forced a smile. "Yeah, sure."

She hesitated and then stepped toward the door. "Alright, let's go then."

CHAPTER SEVENTEEN

THE HOSPITAL SMELLED like sanitizer and plastic. I wrinkled my nose as I walked past the front desk. Ms. Swallow nodded at the woman sitting behind it and motioned toward the hall.

They must have known each other because all she got was a courtesy wave before the woman returned to the computer on her desk.

I let Ms. Swallow lead me down the hallway. She hesitated in front of room 43B. I studied it as she reached up and knocked.

The door opened and a nurse came out.

"Oh, hello. You must be Josh's wife and"—she glanced around to look at me—"his daughter?"

I watched as Ms. Swallow's cheeks turned pink. "I'm not his wife," she whispered.

"But I'm his daughter. Can I see him?" I asked, stepping around Ms. Swallow and nodding toward the door.

The nurse nodded. "Of course."

I didn't wait for Ms. Swallow. Instead, I entered the room. The farther I walked, the slower my gait became. Did I want to see him? Pain gripped my heart as realization sank in.

I could have lost Dad today. It could have been a lot worse than a broken leg and a concussion. And if he had died, where would I be? With Mom? I scoffed. That was a joke.

No. If Dad had died, I would be alone. Like *alone*, alone. As the weight of the day and this realization settled in around me, I felt tears sting my eyes.

I couldn't believe that I had been so angry before. I had lied to Dad about where I was going and who I was spending time with. And the stupid part of all of this was that I'd tried to trade the person who cared about me for a guy who dropped me the moment things got hard.

Dad was right—boys were trouble. All they did was lead you along and then break your heart. From this moment on, I wasn't going to allow anyone to derail me from what was important. I would never lie to Dad about who I was seeing. I would be upfront and honest. Always.

The clicking of the machines grew louder as I passed the bathroom and saw Dad lying on the hospital bed. His head was wrapped in a bandage. His left leg was raised higher than the other, propped up on a pillow. I sucked in my breath as I studied the white gauze on his leg.

Half his face was scuffed up and puffy. Like he'd landed on it. His eyes were closed, and I contemplated turning around and leaving him to sleep.

If I were honest with myself, I was being a little selfish. I didn't want to see him like this. It broke my heart, even more than it already was. Why hadn't I just gone with him to Pirate's Cove? He wouldn't have been with Ms. Swallow. He wouldn't have been in the crosswalk, where that jerk hit him.

Even though I was inclined to blame myself, when I really thought about it, it was all Ms. Swallow's fault. Why had she even called Dad in the first place? And who had picked that restaurant?

I turned to glare at her as she walked in and touched Dad's arm, the arm that had an IV sticking out of it.

"Why are you here?" I asked, wincing at the bite in my tone.

If I'd learned anything these past few days, it was that Dad and I were better off alone. All we needed was each other. He didn't need Ms. Swallow, and I didn't need Tyson. If we could just go back to the way things were, I'd be happy, and Dad...well, I'm sure he'd be happy as well.

Ms. Swallow's gaze made its way over to me. I must have had a menacing look because her eyes widened. "Your dad wanted me to bring you here," she said, her voice low, as if she'd felt the full weight of my accusation without me having to say anything.

I felt like I should smile and say it was fine, that she could totally stay. Instead, I opened my mouth and said, "Well, you did that. You can go home now."

I couldn't meet her gaze, so I focused on grabbing a nearby chair and pulling it toward Dad's bed. Once I'd settled in, I glanced over to where she still stood.

She'd dropped her attention back to Dad's face. His eyes were still closed. That man could sleep through an alien invasion. Her fingers still lingered on his arm, and for some reason, that really bugged me.

"I'll let you know when he's up," I lied. I folded my arms. Was she really going to make me say it? I had the power here. After all, I was family and she wasn't.

Thankfully, she took the hint and nodded as she shouldered her purse. "Sorry. You're right. You should have some time with your dad." She tucked a curl behind her ear. "I'll have my uncle tow your dad's car here so you have something to drive. His keys are most likely in his belongings." She nodded toward the closet on my right.

"Sounds good," I said. I really needed her to leave before I broke down. I didn't want to give her another reason to stick around.

She sighed and then took a few steps toward the door. "Don't hesitate to call me if you need anything."

I hated how nice she was being to me. It made disliking her that much harder. "Yep," I said, emphasizing the *p*.

She took one last look around then walked out into the hall, shutting the door behind her.

Now alone, I let my gaze sweep the room and, every so often, I let it linger on Dad's face. Regret and anger built up in my chest as I studied him. Why was I such a terrible daughter? I was ridiculous if I thought it was okay to run around with a boy behind Dad's back.

He deserved better than that. He'd always protected me. Why was this any different?

Exhaustion overtook me, so I brought up my foot and rested it on my seat. I used my knee as a tool to prop my head up, I relaxed and let my eyes close.

"Tiny?"

I bolted up from where I had hunched over. I winced as the crick in my neck tightened. "Dad?" I asked.

He was sitting up in his bed with a tired expression. When I met his gaze, his eyes widened. "How did you get here?"

I rubbed the knot in my shoulders with one hand while I dragged the chair closer to him with the other. "Ms. Swallow brought me."

He glanced around the room. "Angelica? Where is she?"

A bit of jealousy crept up into my chest. Why did he care where she was? Hadn't he told me that relationships were dumb? We were better off without them. "She said she had things to take care of," I said flatly.

I tried to ignore the hurt expression that flashed over his face. "Oh," he said.

Add that to the list of things that made me a horrible daughter. I knew that Dad was completely smitten by Ms. Swallow, and yet, here I was, trying to push them apart. Then I shook that thought away. I was helping Dad. After all, wasn't that what he'd been doing for me all along?

"But I'm here." I gave him a hopeful smile. That seemed to appease him, and he returned it with a smile of his own.

"That makes me so happy," he said, reaching out to grasp my hand.

I held his hand, and before I could stop myself, the words "I'm sorry" tumbled from my lips.

He shook his head. "No, I'm sorry. I should have never let something like that get in the way of our relationship. You didn't know that boys would be at that party, and you've never broken my rules before. I should have trusted you." He steadied his expression. "I trust you, Destiny."

Wow. He went full name and everything. He only did that when he was serious.

I swallowed, trying to ignore the lump in my throat. He trusted me. He thought that I would never lie to him. Ugh, I was a terrible daughter.

But the truth was, I wasn't ever going to lie to him again. I just wasn't ready to tell him that I had lied in the past. Or that I'd snuck around with Tyson, one of the guys he forbade me to even look at. And I was definitely not going to tell him that I just might have fallen in love with Tyson.

Love.

Just saying that word in my mind caused my already

hemorrhaging heart to squeeze. Why did I even think that word? It would be easier to get over Tyson if it was just a dumb crush. But if I loved him?

I halted that thought. Nope. I wasn't going to dwell on that. If I had any chance at getting over him, I had to stop thinking about our time together. Or how he made me feel.

I inwardly groaned. I needed to talk about something else.

"So, what are we going to do once we break you out of here?" I asked, grabbing a nearby pillow and hugging it in my lap.

"Well, I was telling Angelica about the cabin we used to rent up on Lake George. Remember that?"

Anger settled in my gut. "Ms. Swallow? Really, Dad?"

He glanced over at me. "What? Don't you like her?"

"She's nice, I guess. For a teacher." I raised my eyebrows, hoping he'd get the hint.

He didn't. He looked as oblivious as ever. "And?"

"I guess I just can't believe that you want to let this stranger enter our lives like this. I mean, come on, haven't you told me that relationships are doomed from the start? That all they do is end with you brokenhearted? To avoid them like you would the plague?" My voice began to rise as agitation boiled up inside of me.

His eyes widened. "I said those things?"

He's in a hospital bed, Destiny. Cut him some slack.

I let out my breath slowly and settled back into my chair. I didn't have to get all worked up. I just needed to remind him why he hated relationships. I needed to bring up Mom.

"I just figured that since Mom pretty much ripped your heart out and abandoned me, she'd ruined you from wanting a relationship ever again." I picked at the fraying cuff of my sleeve, trying to act like I didn't care what his response would be.

He was quiet before he let out his breath. It sounded like he was getting ready to tell a long story and needed to prime his lungs. "Well, if that's what you think of me, then I've failed you."

I stared at him. "What?"

"You mother hurt me, yes. But that doesn't mean that I don't ever want a relationship again. And I most certainly want you to find a guy and marry him."

My eyes bugged.

"Some day *way* in the future." He winced as he raised his arm, waving his hand.

"Really? 'Cause I did not get that from the last few years of my life. I thought you hated everything about marriage and dating." I folded my arms. Nothing like finding out your dad wanted love for himself, even though he forbade it for you.

He sighed and reached up to gingerly rub his temple. "Can we talk about this another time? I'm tired."

I nodded. "Yeah. Sure."

He lay back onto his bed and closed his eyes. Five minutes later, he was snoring.

I pulled out my phone only to find that I had a message from Tyson. My heart took off galloping. Part of me wished so bad that he had texted to tell me he was an idiot, that we should be together no matter what. Actually, not part of me —all of me wished for that.

But I couldn't stand another heartbreaking statement from him. So I deleted the message. I really didn't want to hear from him ever again.

After ten minutes of sitting in Dad's room with nothing to do, I got up and wandered out to the hall. After asking a nearby nurse where the cafeteria was, I followed her directions and got in line to order.

It felt good to do something mind numbing. Something that I didn't really need to think about. Because if there was one thing I was sure of, it was that I needed to stop thinking for the day. Or maybe the month.

CHAPTER EIGHTEEN

I SPENT the weekend with Dad at the hospital. It was better than being at home, where I was alone. The nurses were funny, and after a good night's sleep, Dad was more awake and aware of his surroundings. We laughed and played some hospital-provided boardgames.

It was interesting. Most of them had missing pieces, so we had to improvise.

We kept our conversation light and fluffy. Apparently, Dad had picked up on the fact that *Ms. Swallow* and *relationship* had become trigger words for me, so he stayed clear of both.

If she-that-shall-not-be-named called, Dad didn't tell me.

She did, however, text me once to let me know that Dad's car was parked in the lot behind the hospital and how to find it.

So when I walked into Chemistry on Monday morning, I really wasn't sure what to expect. Was she going to be nice to me? Mean?

Thankfully, the entire school had heard what had happened to Coach Davis, so I was peppered with condolences and questions about his recovery. It helped take my mind off the impending doom I was going to experience in Chem. Where Ms. Swallow and Tyson were.

I glanced to my table to see Tyson sitting at it. His gaze was focused on his textbook in front of him. I snorted. He'd finally decided to give a crap about his grade—now that I wasn't going to be around to hold his hand.

I still wanted to be there for him. But just seeing the way his shaggy hair fell across his forehead, or the way he furrowed his brow as he read, was enough to cause my heart to pick up speed and tears to brim my lids.

I couldn't do this. I had to get out of here.

Turning on my heel, I ran smack-dab into Ms. Swallow. Her eyes widened as she took in my expression.

"Are you okay, Destiny?" she asked, grabbing my elbow and pulling me out into the hall as the final bell rang.

I nodded, chewing my lip. There was no way I could spill to her what had happened over the weekend. I couldn't tell her that I'd fallen for the quarterback—Dad's sworn enemy. She'd run off and tell him in a heartbeat. Get Dad to stop trusting me so that she could swoop in and take my place.

"Is it your dad, honey? Are you worried about him?" She

reached out and rested her hand on my arm. "Because I talked to him this morning, and they are going to release him tomorrow evening. I'm picking him up."

My frustration turned to rage as her words sank in. "You're what?" I asked. I was shouting now, but I didn't care.

Dad hadn't changed. Even after our conversation, where I'd basically told him that I didn't want him dating Ms. Swallow, he'd gone ahead, behind my back, and talked to her.

Ms. Swallow raised her eyebrows. "I'm sorry. I thought he told you."

I narrowed my eyes. "Don't you think you've done enough? If it hadn't been for you, Dad would have never been in that crosswalk." I pointed my finger at her chest. "This is all your fault, and I want you to stay away from me and my dad." My voice was shaking as hard as my hand was. I hadn't felt this betrayed and hurt since Mom had pulled out of the driveway with Pedro in the front seat.

Ms. Swallow hesitated. I could see she had words lingering on the tip of her tongue, but then she nodded. "You're right. I never took into consideration what this might do to you, Destiny. I decided to never date a student's parent, and I guess I just rationalized it away saying he was more another teacher than a parent." She sighed. "I'm sorry if I hurt your feelings."

I scoffed, shocked that she was being so nice about this. It was making it hard not to hate her. She was genuine and cared. That was a lot more than I'd gotten from any other woman in my life.

"Thanks," I said, my voice softening. Actually, my whole body was relaxing, making me feel light-headed. I leaned against the lockers for support. It was as if the realization of what had happened this weekend came crashing down around me, and my body was reacting from the weight.

"Destiny, are you going to be okay?" she asked, reaching out to touch my arm.

I nodded. "Yeah. I'm just really overwhelmed."

"Maybe you should go home."

"No," I blurted out. That was the last place I wanted to be. "No, I'm okay. I—I just was wondering if I could swap lab partners. Tyson and I..." I eyed her, sizing her up. Could I trust her? I pushed the doubt from my mind. She'd already kept my previous secrets, there was no reason for her to spill anything to Dad now. "We had a falling out, and I think with what happened this weekend with my dad, I'm just not up to being around him right now."

"Of course. I'll switch you and Betsy."

Relief flooded my chest as I pushed off the lockers and followed her into her classroom. The noise dropped off to whispers as we entered. I could feel Tyson's gaze on me, but I kept my eyes trained to the floor while Ms. Swallow called Betsy up to the front and explained to her what was happening.

After Betsy agreed and gathered her things, I made my way over to her lab table and sat down next to Sam, my new partner. Thankfully, I was behind Tyson, so I didn't have to worry about him staring at me. It felt oddly comforting, being in control like this.

The rest of class, I only let my gaze linger on the back of his head five times. I kept count in my head. One of those times, he glanced behind him and met my gaze—which I dropped instantly.

By the time the bell rang, I was exhausted and ready to get out of there. I didn't wait around for anyone—I was the first person out the door. But as soon as I got out into the hall, I was stopped by a few football players who wanted a Boss update. I explained to them what had happened and that he was expected to come back to school by the end of the week.

They nodded and patted my back, pushing me forward a few inches, as they passed by me. I swallowed and glanced toward Ms. Swallow's room. Had Tyson left yet?

I put my head down and headed to English. I needed to stop thinking about him right now if I was going to survive the rest of the year. Tyson and I were done. Finished.

When I got to the lunchroom, I'd successfully pushed him from my mind. Instead of thinking about the way his eyes lit up when he talked about Cori or the way he stared at me in an open and unabashed way, I'd resorted to singing *ninety-nine bottles of beer on the wall*.

Just as I got to ninety, a familiar hand grabbed my elbow, and I was pulled into the supply closet.

I didn't have to turn around to know that Tyson would

be standing behind me. But when I did, my heart leapt into my throat. His expression was one of concern with his lips downturned. When I met his gaze, he ran his hand through his hair.

"What do you want, Tyson?" I asked, forcing my voice to come out strong.

He glanced at me and then to the floor. "I—um—" I watched his shoulders rise as he took a deep breath. He wasn't even sure why he'd pulled me in here.

"I'm fine. If you wanted to make sure you didn't break this naive girl's heart, let me put your worry at ease. I'm just fine."

Stop saying fine, Destiny. He'll know you're most certainly not fine.

But I couldn't let him know that he was breaking my heart, that being in this room—breathing the same air as him —was killing me. Slowly and painfully.

"How's your dad?" he finally asked, glancing up at me.

He was hurting. It was written all over his face. He was in pain, and that realization gripped my chest and squeezed until I could barely breathe. "He's fine," I whispered. I wasn't going to let him win. I would be the stronger person. After all, he had dumped me.

He nodded and then slowed. "And you?"

Hadn't we already covered this? I'd told him about fifty times that I was fine. But I doubted he was even listening. He was too preoccupied with whatever he wasn't saying.

"Listen, if you're feeling guilty about what happened on

Saturday, don't. It was good, what you said, and ending this"
—I waved between his chest and my own—"whatever it is,
was smart. I'd promised my dad that I wasn't going to date,
and I was an idiot to think that lying to him so that I could
be with you was a good idea. If something really bad had
happened to my dad while we were together, I would have
never been able to forgive myself."

I forced a smile. It felt more like a jack-o-lantern grin
than anything.

A wave of sadness passed over Tyson's face. I tried not
to let that sway my resolve.

Standing in this room with him one more minute just
might kill me. Just being around him was breaking my
resolve. I stepped past him, toward the door.

He reached out, grabbing my arm before I could leave. I
was only inches from him. My breath caught in my throat as
I hesitated. I knew, in a moment, I was going to have to look
up at him. To have a front-row seat to his pain.

"It's okay," I whispered, raising my gaze to meet his.

Tyson swallowed hard and then glanced over at me.
"I'm so sorry," he said.

I nodded. "I know."

We stood there in silence. I swore I could hear the
beating of our hearts. I would have given anything to be able
to tell him that I loved him. That I didn't want to walk away.
But I couldn't. It wasn't fair to him, and it was most certainly
not fair to me.

I patted his hand then opened the door and left. As I

walked down the hall toward English, I tried hard to fight back the tears. I guess one nice thing about having Dad in the hospital was that most people who saw me blubbering would assume it was because of him and not Tyson.

I walked into English and realized that I couldn't do this. Two nights of sleeping propped up on the chair in Dad's room plus the emotional baggage I was carrying around had taken its toll on me. All I wanted to do was crawl onto one of those leather cots in the nurse's room and take a nap.

So that was what I did. Mr. Jones didn't have a problem letting me go. It was probably because I looked like I was on the brink of breaking down. And as soon as I walked into the office, all the students got out of my way as I walked past them and into the nurse's room.

I headed straight over to the first cot, and I curled up on it. I closed my eyes as Mrs. Tate took my temperature and blood pressure and then told me to rest. I nodded and closed my eyes, letting sleep take over me.

CHAPTER NINETEEN

I WALKED into Dad's room that night feeling a bit more refreshed after my six-period nap in Mrs. Tate's office. She woke me up a few times to see if I wanted to go home, but I refused, telling her that my house was too quiet. She seemed to understand and left me alone until the final bell rang.

I tried not to think about all the schoolwork I was missing. I was banking on the fact that most of the teachers would have heard about Dad and would cut me some slack.

Dad was sitting in his wheelchair with a cast on his leg. He was dressed in sweatpants with one leg cut off. He had a t-shirt on and was watching a basketball game. I reveled in the sound of him yelling at the screen. He was back to his normal self.

"Hey, Dad," I said, dumping my backpack on the floor and collapsing on the chair that had become my bed.

"Hey, Tiny," he said, waving toward me.

He was fixated on the game, so I stood and wandered around the room. People had sent flowers and cards, and I picked up a few to read them. They were from fellow teachers or parents of players.

When I found a box of chocolates, I grabbed them and made my way back to the chair. Just as I sat down, the commercials started up.

That broke Dad's concentration, and he turned to smile at me. "How was school?"

"Good," I mumbled through a bite of caramel-filled chocolate.

"Find the chocolate Mrs. Benson sent?"

"Yep. It's delicious," I said, popping another one in my mouth.

He laughed. "Glad my broken leg can bring happiness to someone." Then his expression grew serious. "Was Ms. Swallow there today?"

Frustration rose up in my chest. Why was he asking about her? I wanted to say that he'd betrayed me by asking Ms. Swallow to take him home tomorrow. "Why? I thought we'd decided that you were done with her."

He furrowed his brow. "I never decided that."

I scoffed and shoved another chocolate into my mouth. "Yes, you did."

He studied me. "What's with you?"

It angered me that he couldn't figure out what was happening. I had to give up the one guy that cared about me because of his ridiculous rules, and yet he could go gallivanting around with my chemistry teacher like it was no big deal.

Out of annoyance, I grabbed the remote and changed the channel.

"Hey!" Dad said, glancing over at me. "I was watching that."

I shrugged. Before he retorted, a news anchor appeared on the screen.

"This weekend, a contest was held at Disneyland. They were celebrating the fact that the park has now served eight hundred million guests. To commemorate this amazing feat, they were giving away year-long passes to the eight hundred millionth guest."

The screen flashed to the picture of Tyson, Cori...and me.

I swallowed so hard that a piece of chocolate got lodged in my throat. I coughed and coughed. Dad glanced over at me, and I couldn't quite read his reaction.

"You okay?" he asked.

I nodded as tears formed. Finally, the chocolate worked its way down, and I was able to drink away the tickle. The news anchor talked about how we won the passes and to contact the park for more information. Then she moved on to a shooting that happened earlier that day.

Dad and I had stopped listening. Instead, I was focused on Dad and what he was thinking.

He was quiet before he turned and focused his attention

on me. "Wanna explain to me why you were in a picture with Tyson and his sister this weekend?"

Anger and shame coursed through me. I was hurt that he had the gall to accuse me when he himself was seeing someone behind my back. But I also knew that I'd made a mistake. I had lied, and no amount of blame was going to cover up that fact.

"I've been seeing Tyson," I blurted out. Well, that was one way of addressing the issue.

Dad's eyes widened. "You've what?"

I swallowed. "I've been seeing Tyson. Ms. Swallow put us together as lab partners, and he needed help, so he asked me if I would tutor him. I knew how you felt, but I also didn't want to say no." I let out my remaining breath, trying to gauge his reaction.

"You were studying chemistry at Disneyland?"

I shook my head. "No. It started out me helping him, and then we picked up his mom at a bar." Dad's mouth dropped open. Crap, I probably wasn't supposed to say anything. "He probably doesn't want you to know that," I muttered under my breath.

Too late. I was already this far in, I might as well finish it. "We started hanging out, and he was at the party I went to with Rebecca. He has to take care of his little sister, so we left the party and went to his house so he could put her to bed." Why couldn't I shut up? Dad didn't ask for every single detail.

I suppose I'd been holding so much of this in that it felt

good to finally get it all out. Thankfully I had enough control to keep from spilling about the kiss.

"He asked me to go along with him and his sister to Disneyland. I guess their mom is a piece of work, and she's more drunk than anything and couldn't go with them. And you know, since Mom..." My voice trailed off.

Exhaustion overcame me, and I flopped back on the chair, unable to look at Dad anymore. I hated the disappointment that was written all over his face. I hated that I'd lied. I hated all of this.

"Destiny," he said, taking the time to say every syllable in my name.

I covered my eyes with my elbow. "Yeah?"

"I'm sorry."

I sat up. What did he just say? I glanced over at him, and he had an apologetic look on his face. I studied him. Was this a joke? "For what?" I'd been the one to break his rule. I'd been the one to lie.

He sighed and fiddled with the fraying hem of his pants turned shorts. "For not being the dad you needed."

A lump formed in my throat. "Don't say that. You're the best kind of dad. You take care of me. You're there for me. You never abandoned me." My voice broke and trailed off to a whisper.

"But I dragged you along with the pain I've held onto ever since your mom left. You didn't deserve that. You needed someone to teach you how to forgive. How to move on. And I didn't do any of that." He blew out his breath as if what he'd said had been weighing on him for a long time.

I sat up, trying to digest what he was saying. Did he understand why I'd lied to him? And he wasn't mad? Who took my dad, and what did they replace him with? Because the man sitting in a wheelchair over by the window certainly wasn't him.

And then it all became clear. He liked Ms. Swallow. And he knew that he was being hypocritical by telling me I couldn't date Tyson. He was changing his tune so he could date Ms. Swallow.

A brick weight sat on my chest. I'd never felt so betrayed and angry before. This had nothing to do with me or how he had failed me. It had everything to do with the fact that he wanted something and I was standing in his way.

Why couldn't he have had this revelation days ago? Before Tyson broke up with me, saying that he couldn't be with me because of the liability I brought? Just my luck, it happened after I might have had a chance with a guy I cared about. Because right now, there was no way Tyson would touch me with a ten-foot pole.

I'd broken his heart.

"Is this because of Ms. Swallow?" I asked, narrowing my eyes. "Because no matter how you feel about me dating, I will never feel right about you dating my chemistry teacher."

Dad's eyes widened, but I didn't let him talk. Truth was, I needed to get out of this room and away from my two-faced dad. The person who claimed to want to protect me, but then changed his mind the minute it became inconvenient for him.

"I have to go," I said, grabbing my backpack and heading toward the door.

"Wait. Where are you going?" he called after me.

I tried to shove away the guilt I felt when I saw him struggle to push his wheelchair over to me. I couldn't feel sorry for him right now. My anger toward him and Tyson was the only thing keeping me sane. If I let it go, I just might crumble into a pile of ash.

"Away from you," I said and headed out into the hall. I didn't need him or want him to follow after me. I needed some time to myself to just think.

I rounded the corner and ran smack-dab into Tyson's chest. His hands wrapped around my arms as he glanced down at me. A look of concern passed over his face. I forced the tears to retreat. He couldn't see me cry.

"He's in there." I waved behind me as I passed by the entire football team.

I heard Tyson mumble something that sounded like "I'll catch up with you," but I didn't wait to see if I'd heard right. Instead, I got to the stairs and pushed open the door. I didn't want to wait for the elevator.

Tyson must have not realized my escape route because I found myself alone when I got outside. Which I was grateful for. Right?

Shaking off my ridiculous thoughts, I headed straight to the place where I'd parked Dad's car. His beat-up, blue

Chevy sat between two white BMWs. I clicked the key fob that I carried around in my backpack and heard the beep as the car doors unlocked.

"Hey, Tiny. Wait up."

I heard Tyson call my name from across the parking lot, but I didn't want to wait. I needed to get out of there.

I pulled open the driver's door but stopped when Tyson's hand reached out and caught it. I growled and pushed against his arm. When he didn't budge, I pushed away from him and met him with the full extent of my anger.

"Why won't you just leave me alone?" I asked. Crap. I couldn't keep my tears in check. One escaped and slid down my cheek.

When he didn't say anything, I glanced up to see him studying me.

I wiped at my cheeks, cursing the fact that he was so calm and I was such a mess. Well, apparently, he wasn't as devastated by our sort-of-not-really breakup as I was.

"Is that what you want?" he finally asked.

Was it wrong that I hated how caring he looked at this moment? Like the only thing that mattered to him was my happiness. It was something that I longed for and hated at the same time.

"Yes," I said, but it didn't come out as confident as I had hoped. Instead, my voice sounded small. A little like the lies I'd been telling since school started.

He dipped down to meet my gaze. "Really?"

Oh, he wanted the real answer. Well, if he wanted honesty, then no, I didn't want him to leave me alone. As corny as it sounded, he was a part of me and leaving would create a giant, Tyson-sized hole in my heart.

I blew out my breath and folded my arms. "What do you want?"

Good, Destiny. Turn the question on him. Make him as vulnerable as he made you.

Tyson leaned forward, and I could feel his presence wash over me. Despite my efforts, my heart pounded harder.

"The truth?" he asked.

Heat raced to my cheeks, but I kept my cool as I nodded. "Sure. 'Cause I'm not really sure how things have changed since two days ago when you told me that we couldn't be together."

Except they had. Dad pretty much gave me his blessing to date Tyson so he could date Ms. Swallow. But Tyson didn't know that, and I wasn't sure I wanted to know what he'd do with that information.

As if the mention of our time together at Disneyland was the key to my release, he pulled back.

"I..." His voice trailed off as if he wasn't sure what to say.

Instead of waiting for his answer, I took this moment, when his guard was down, to get into the car.

"I thought so," I said as I shut the door and started the engine.

He stepped to the side as I pulled out of the parking spot

and drove away. Just as I turned onto the main road, the dam broke and tears fell in huge droplets down my cheeks.

I hated how I felt. I hated how I left things with Dad. And now, I hated how I left things with Tyson.

But what I had done was necessary if I was going to protect myself. There was no way I could allow another person into my life who could hurt me. I just needed to survive.

CHAPTER TWENTY

NOTHING GOT BETTER over the next few days. If anything, they got worse. Dad was back and crankier than ever. I tried to tell myself it was because he was trying to maneuver the crazy-packed halls with a wheelchair, but I knew better.

It had everything to do with his promise that he would end things with Ms. Swallow. He even admitted that he hadn't been fair, treating me that way.

I had nodded and told him I was grateful for his honesty and the fact that he saw the hypocrisy in it all. That hadn't made his mood any better. He was crabbier at practice, making all the players—especially Tyson—run laps in the lingering summer heat.

I sat in the shade, watching the guys run back and forth. I raised my hand and squinted as I saw Rebecca cheering in the neighboring field. I hadn't really been able to talk to her since Brutus's party over the weekend. She'd been really busy with cheer and her blossoming relationship with Colten.

I didn't agree with it, but what could I do? She was a big girl and could make her own choices. I, on the other hand, was in the market for a life coach. I was done making my own decisions.

After practice, all the guys except Tyson came up to the table and grabbed a glass of water. Once they were hydrated, I began to clean up.

To my relief, Rebecca came running over. Beads of sweat had formed on her brow, and she swiped them away. I wished I had her kind of elegance. Even her sweat looked dainty.

"Hey, Des," she said, grabbing the remaining glass of water and downing it.

"Bec," I said, wrapping her into a hug—sweat and all.

She laughed. "You don't want to touch me. I'm gross."

I shook my head as I held on. I needed this. I needed at least one person in my life who wasn't disappointed by my decisions.

She let me hang onto her for a minute longer before I dropped my arms and she pulled away. "Everything okay?" she asked.

I sighed as I started to take down the table. "No. It's not."

And that was the truth.

"Oh, no. What happened?"

So I told her. Everything.

Her eyes grew wide at certain points, and her lips turned down at others. When I told her about the mind-bending kiss we'd shared at his house, her lips parted as her jaw dropped.

But when I got to the part that involved the hospital, she grew still. As if she were trying to analyze what I had just told her.

When I finished, I waited for her to say something. I really wanted her to agree with me. To tell me that I had every right to break up my dad and Ms. Swallow and to leave Tyson standing in the parking lot, alone.

"So?" I asked, looking at her expectantly.

She grabbed the water jug and bag of cups. I picked up the table, and we started making our way down to the school.

"So, what?"

I sighed. Loud. "So what do you think?"

She glanced over at me. "Does it matter?"

Frustration boiled up inside of me. "Yeah, kind of."

"Why?"

Why was she acting so therapist-y on me? "Because you're my best friend. I want to know what you think." I left out the part where I wanted her to agree with me, because if she did, it would feel fake.

"You want honesty, Des?"

I nodded.

"I think you're acting stupid."

I scoffed, setting the table down to look at her. "Excuse me?"

She turned and sighed. "I didn't mean it like that."

"Well, how did you mean it? There really isn't a different way to interpret *stupid*."

Switching the bag of cups to the hand that held the jug, she pinched the bridge of her nose. "It's just that, I saw you do the same thing when your mom left. You stopped talking to me for months, remember that?"

I narrowed my eyes. I had some vague recollection of that. But I thought it was because she had been busy with cheer. "But you had cheer."

"That was the excuse you told yourself. I was there for you, but you shut me out. You were scared I would leave you too, so you left first."

I studied her. Was that true? I'd kind of blocked out most of that year. If I remembered it, then I would remember the pain that coursed through me when I watched Mom drive away.

I swallowed. I was a horrible friend. "Bec, I'm so sorry."

She shrugged. "You came around eventually. But hearing you talk about Tyson and Ms. Swallow reminds me of how you were back then. How desperately you pushed people away to keep them from hurting you."

"But I let myself care about Tyson. How is that trying to protect myself?" I wanted to tell her that she was crazy. It sounded like she was saying all of this was my fault. When it wasn't. Right?

"You let yourself care for him when you had an out. Your dad's ridiculous rule kept you protected. If push came to shove, you could tell him that your dad would forbid you to date and you could leave. It was a clean break. But when your dad changed his mind, suddenly you had no reason to stay away, and the threat of being hurt became real."

I dragged the table over into the school's shadow and leaned against wall. "Well, what does that have to do with my dad dating Ms. Swallow?"

Rebecca followed and propped herself up right next to me. "Because she's a representation of your mom. If you dad likes her and brings her into your life, there's a chance she could leave you too." Rebecca grew silent, and I felt her gaze on me.

I swallowed hard. The emotional lump made it difficult to talk. I knew what she was saying was true. If Dad got remarried someday and that woman left, I wasn't sure I'd survive that. It would just confirm what I had feared forever. That I was unlovable. That everyone would leave me eventually.

This conversation was good, but it left me with just as many questions as I'd started with. "What do I do now?" I stared down at the grass and dug the toe of my shoe into it.

"What do you mean?" she asked.

"Well, now that we know how screwed up I am and how I sabotaged every relationship I've ever had, what do I do now? How do I"—I drew a circle in the air with my hand—"move forward? Fix this?"

I turned to meet her gaze. Her eyebrows were raised.

"Do you want to fix this?"

Even though fear gripped my heart, the truth was, yes, I wanted to move on. I wanted to be happy. And I wanted those I cared about to be happy. I nodded. "Yeah, I think I do."

She pushed off the wall and smiled over at me. "Alright. Let's start operation Fix Des's Mistakes."

I let out the breath I'd been holding and grabbed the table. "Let's do this."

IT TOOK until Friday to plan operation Fix Des's Mistakes. It also required a lot of negotiation with and bribing of the football team.

I was grateful to have Rebecca by my side. She helped pump me up when I was having a hard day with Dad or remind me why we were doing this when I passed by Tyson in the hall. There was a method to her madness, and I just needed to trust her.

So when I walked into the stadium Friday night, I swallowed down my nerves. I was really going to do this. I was going to put myself out there and allow love back into my life.

Secretly, I hoped that Tyson would come running back to my arms and Dad and Ms. Swallow would make up and pull themselves out of the sour mood they'd been in all week. I was ready to be happy again, and that started with helping those I cared about be happy.

When I approached the bleachers, I saw the section Rebecca and I had cornered off earlier in the day. We'd decided to set up a romantic spot where Dad and Ms. Swallow could watch the game. We'd laid out a blanket and even provided a picnic basket with snacks and some sparkling cider.

Now, we just needed them.

My phone chimed and I glanced down at it. Dad texted me that he was talking with the team and would meet me once the game started. I blew out my breath as I replied back for him to hurry up. I wasn't sure how long Ms. Swallow was going to stay once Rebecca finally got her here.

Which was right now. I could see Rebecca talking to Ms. Swallow and trying to strategically guide her over to our picnic setup.

"I'm just not really in the mood to watch football right now," Ms. Swallow said. I hated the way her lips turned down or how sad she looked. I guess I'd tried to ignore it all week, but she'd been hurt by everything. Probably just as bad as I had been.

I smiled as she approached the bleachers. I wanted this terrible nightmare to be over. I was ready to stop hurting those that I loved.

"Destiny," she said, when her gaze landed on me. "What are you doing here?" Her eyes roamed over the blanket and sectioned-off spot. "What's going on?"

"It was my fault," I blurted out.

Her eyebrows rose. "Excuse me?"

I let out my breath slowly, willing myself to calm down. I had a long night of apologies ahead of me and there was no sense losing my cool now. "My dad breaking up with you. It was my fault. I told him to." It almost hurt to look into her eyes. I knew I would see frustration and anger there, and I thought I had prepared myself for it. But when I met her gaze, I paused.

There wasn't anger or frustration there. Just sympathy. Her lips turned up into a smile. "It's okay, Destiny. Really. I understand why you did it." She leaned closer. "My mom left when I was eight. Dad and Uncle Ted took care of me. It was hard when my dad started dating as well." She puffed up her cheeks before she blew out her breath. "I would never do anything that would come in between you and your dad."

I nodded. "I know. I was—am just scared. Scared of opening up and letting someone in." Well, letting a lot of people in. But it helped to talk about it. Recognizing what I'd done helped break down a part of the wall that surrounded my heart.

She reached out and rested her hand on my shoulder. "Well, that's very brave of you, Destiny. There are many adults who lack that kind of bravery."

Tears pricked my eyes. Hearing someone say I was brave was doing strange things to my insides. It felt good and like a lie at the same time. But, instead of fighting it, I nodded and smiled, letting her compliment wash over me. "Thanks."

She nodded and then reached out, pulling me into a hug. At first, I wanted to pull away, but then I let it happen. I liked Ms. Swallow. She was a good person, and Dad deserved a good person in his life. I was selfish to want to keep her away. Not everyone was evil. Not everyone was Mom.

"What's going on here?" Dad's voice caused us both to jump back.

I glanced over at him with a sheepish expression. "Peace offering?" I said, extending my hand.

Dad's gaze ran over the bleachers and then over to Ms. Swallow, where I swore I saw him blush. Dad. Blushing. *Weird.*

"Angelica," he said, nodding in her direction.

"Joshua," she whispered.

It was strange to watch Dad turn into this bashful schoolboy. Honestly, it kind of creeped me out. I was ready for Dad to start dating; I just didn't want to experience it firsthand. Plus, there was one more person I had to apologize to.

But I needed to hear from Dad's lips that we were cool. So I nodded him over to the edge of the bleachers, and he rolled his wheelchair to meet me.

"Are you sure about this?" he asked. Apparently, he had things he needed to hear from me, too.

"Yeah, I'm sure," I said. "I like Ms. Swallow. And it's

time. You deserve someone special. Someone to take care of you, old man. 'Cause I'm not going to be around forever."

I saw his jaw muscles flinch, and I mentally slapped myself. I was about to ask him if I could date Tyson. I didn't need to be reminding him what that meant for his little girl.

"You know what I mean," I said, hoping my casual attitude helped alleviate any stress he might be feeling about me leaving.

He hesitated and then smiled. "Thanks. That means a lot. And know that if you need to talk to me, you can. I might not always be happy, but I'd rather you be honest with me." He stuck out his hand. "Promise to always tell me the truth?"

I eyed his hand. "Promise not to freak out or make up ridiculous rules?"

I saw him pull his hand back a few inches, considering my request, and then push it forward again. "Deal."

Instead of shaking his hand, I threw my arms around him and squeezed him as tight as I could, with him being in a wheelchair. "I love you, Dad." Tears stung my eyes, and I blinked them away.

"I love you too, Destiny." He pulled back and smiled. "Now, go tell Tyson."

I pulled back and feigned shock. "What? I don't know what you are talking about."

He quirked an eyebrow. "Rule number one, never lie to your father."

I pinched my lips as I thought about it, but then decided

to let that rule stand. I liked it—lying to Dad made me feel horrible, and I was ready to give up that part of my life. So I shot him a sheepish look. "Is that okay?"

His jaw flinched again, and I could tell he was battling his thoughts. Then he blew out his breath and nodded. "Tyson's a good kid. If you like him, then I trust your judgment."

My heart swelled. Was he really giving me his blessing? "I like him," I whispered.

"Then go get him. It's all ready to go."

I rolled my eyes. Could no one keep a secret anymore? I bent down and kissed his cheek, but then I hesitated. "And you go get your girl," I whispered.

He laughed and nodded. "I'll try."

I watched him roll away. Happiness and fear conflicted in my chest as I saw him approach Ms. Swallow. Her smile widened when she saw him, and they began to talk.

Feeling satisfied that I'd accomplished the first step of my plan, I turned toward the back of the bleachers and took a breath. On to the second step—Tyson.

CHAPTER TWENTY-ONE

THE ROAR of the crowd set my nerves on edge as I stood just off the field, where the football team would run out from behind the stadium. There was no way I was going to be able to pull this off.

I swallowed and glanced over at Rebecca, who was talking to Colton. She'd convinced him to come help. I still wasn't sure what the story was there, and I felt like a horrible friend for not knowing.

I shook my head. I couldn't worry about that right now. I needed to focus on Tyson and what I wanted to tell him. Then I'd corner Rebecca and make her spill the story.

The announcer's voice boomed from the speakers as he began building up to introducing the players. I took some short, spastic breaths, hoping it would help calm me. It didn't. What was wrong with me?

I signaled over to Rebecca, who smiled and nodded. I

ran over to her and grabbed the edge of the rolled-up sign, pulling it across the entrance to the field and waiting. I really hoped that the football team would remember what we'd talked about.

After the announcer finished talking about all the Panther's accomplishments, there was a roar from the football team that echoed through the stadium. I held my breath as I waited for them to appear.

Well, actually, if the football team did it right, for Tyson to appear.

And he did. He held his helmet in his hand as he came into view. He looked a bit confused as he kept glancing behind him. Someone must have been just out of sight, waving him forward.

When his gaze landed on me, I thought my heart would burst from my chest and take off galloping across the field. He moved over to the sign I held out, similar to the ones that the team had run through in the past. Except, this one said two words, **I'm Sorry.**

He hesitated, and my breath caught in my throat. What was he going to do? I wouldn't be surprised if he turned around and ran away from me.

So when he did, I was grateful Rebecca and I had a game plan.

I glanced over at her and shook my head. She gave me an encouraging look and then motioned for the cheer team to make their way over to the stadium, where they began chanting and getting the crowd pumped up.

They were going to buy me five minutes until the game started. I needed to find Tyson and tell him that I'd made a mistake.

I took off after him. He wasn't going to be able to get very far. I passed by the team, who shouted out encouraging words to me, but I wasn't really listening. I was focused on Tyson.

Thankfully, I found him leaning against a support pole for the bleachers. The same spot we'd talked a week ago. I sighed, thinking about that weekend. Everything we'd shared together. I wanted to share all my weekends with him.

"Tyson," I said. He stiffened. I hated what my presence was doing to him. Did he really hate me that much? "I'm sorry," I whispered to his back.

He was quiet for a moment before he nodded. "I got that."

I closed my eyes, willing him to turn around. "I was scared," I said, keeping my eyes shut. I needed to get these words out, and if he rejected me after that, so be it. At least I put myself out there.

"Why?"

Shivers raced across my skin. He sounded closer. I swallowed as I opened my eyes to see him standing a foot away, studying me.

Tears formed on my lids when I met his gaze. He was hurting—just as much as I was. I cleared my throat, forcing my emotions down. "Because I was an idiot."

He raised his eyebrows. "And?"

"And, I should have told you when Dad said we could be together."

He hesitated. "When did he say that?"

Great. What was I doing? "When he saw our picture on the news at the hospital."

He held up his hand. "You've known it was okay for us to be together since then?"

I nodded slowly. "Yes."

"And you're waiting until right now to tell me?" He ran his hands through his hair. "Why?"

"I guess I wanted to tell you in a big romantic gesture?"

He jabbed his thumb over his shoulder. "The sign?"

I nodded and stepped closer to him. "That and telling you in front of everyone. No more closets."

He studied me. "What did you want to tell me?"

"That I was sorry."

He took a step closer to me. "And?"

I shot him a surprised look. "What makes you think there's more?"

He chuckled. I loved the sound of it. It was familiar. "Oh, there's always more. It's the Blake charm," he said.

I scoffed and started to turn. He reached out and grabbed my hand, pulling me towards him. "Can I confess something or is this Tiny's confessional?"

"Operation," I corrected, letting him wrap his arm around my waist.

"Operation?"

I nodded. "Yeah, Bec called it operation Fix Des's Mistakes."

He smiled when I placed my hands on his chest. Even though he had shoulder pads on, I pretended that I could feel his heart beating and that it was pounding as hard as mine.

"And what was your mistake?" he asked, dipping down to catch my gaze.

"That I let you go before I told you how I felt."

He leaned closer until his forehead rested on mine. "And how do you feel?"

"I like you," I whispered.

He drew back. "That's all?"

I widened my eyes. "Yes? Why? How do you feel?"

His lips drew up in a half-smile. "I believe this is your operation, not mine."

I pursed my lips and narrowed my eyes at him. He was going to make me say it first. Blast him. I opened my lips, but before I could say anything, a whistle blew from the field, and Tyson straightened. He shot me an apologetic look.

"Gotta go, Tiny." He bent down and brushed his lips on my cheek.

I swallowed as he let me go and started running toward the opening to the field. It was now or never.

"I love you," I shouted after his retreating frame.

He must have heard me because he stopped and then slowly turned around. "What?" he asked, raising his hand to his ear.

Heat radiated from my cheeks. "I love you," I said again.

He smiled and jogged back toward me. "I'm sorry, did you say something?" He was inches from me, dipping down until his ear was right next to my lips.

"I love you," I whispered.

One of his arms wrapped around my waist and pulled me close. With his other hand, he cradled my cheek and ran his thumb over my lips.

"I love you, too," he whispered and then bent down and pressed his lips to mine.

Fireworks exploded across my skin. I ran my hands up his shoulders and entwined them into his hair. He chuckled and wrapped both arms around me, picking me up and spinning me around.

In that moment, nothing mattered. Not Dad or my horrible mother. Not Ms. Swallow or Rebecca. It was just me and Tyson, and I didn't need anything else.

When he set me back down, his expression turned serious. "Are you ready for this? For us?" he asked.

I nodded. "Yes."

He kissed both of my cheeks, my nose, and my forehead before he found his way back to my lips. "Good," he said when he pulled back. "Because I am too."

EPILOGUE

I STOOD in front of my mirror in my room, staring at my reflection. I felt like a dork, dressed in more taffeta and polyester than I had in my entire life combined. But, I'd promised Cori that I would go dressed as a princess for Halloween, and I didn't want to disappoint her.

Things were going well in Tyson's family. His mom went to rehab for a week, and his aunt came to take care of Cori. That allowed him to finally start making it to practice on time and catch up on his missed chemistry work.

I loved seeing this relaxed side of him. He was finally getting to act like a senior high schooler.

I grabbed a bobby pin and tucked an escaping curl back up. Ms. Swallow had insisted that she do my hair. Things were still strange around the house, but both her and Dad knew that I needed time to get used to it, so they made sure to give me my space.

I wouldn't ever admit it to anyone, but I loved having her around. She was amazing and made the best cinnamon rolls ever. Plus, she helped calm Dad down when I accidentally showed up for curfew a few minutes late.

I liked having her on my side.

There was a soft knock on the door. I turned and said, "Come in."

The door handle turned and the door swung open. Tyson stood in my hallway dressed as Prince Charming. He even had the foam sword tucked into his belt. His eyes widened as he stared at me.

"You look beautiful," he said, making his way over to me and pulling me into a hug.

I giggled as I pressed my lips against his.

"What's rule number one?" Dad called from down the hall.

I sighed. Dad and his rules. "No bedrooms," I called back.

I gave Tyson an exasperated look, and we shuffled out to the hallway.

"Thank you," Dad called back.

I sighed, wrapping my arms around Tyson's neck and pulling him down for another kiss. "You look handsome," I said when I pulled back.

He grinned. "That was kind of what I was going for."

I glanced around. "Where's Cori?"

He nodded toward the stairs. "She's showing Angelica her dress."

I cringed. Ms. Swallow had been asking me to call her by her first name for a while now, but I couldn't bring myself to do it. "She got to you too?" I asked, rolling my eyes at him.

He shrugged. "Hey, I want to be a part of your life for a long time. So sue me if I want your family to like me."

My heart skipped a beat at his confession. He wanted to be in my life for a long time? Was it wrong that it made me ridiculously giddy to hear that?

I kissed him again. "Good."

He pressed his forehead against mine. "But your happiness always comes first."

"And mine," Cori's voice grew louder as she appeared at the top of the stairs.

"Of course, yours too," he said, reaching out and catching her as she ran into his arms. After he heaved her onto his hip, he kissed her cheek.

I joined in on the hug, allowing the feeling of completeness to wash over me. Sure, my life wasn't perfect. But right now, it was pretty dang close.

"Thanks for taking a chance on me," I whispered.

Tyson's lips drew closer to my ear. "Of course," he said.

I rose up and kissed him.

"Blegh," Cori said, wiggling from his grasp.

I laughed and glanced down at her. "Ready to get some candy?"

She nodded. "Ready."

***

Thank you so much for reading Tyson and Tiny's story. I hope you enjoyed breaking the first rule of love, you can't date the coach's daughter.

If you LOVED this book, feel free to grab the NEXT book in the Rules of LOVE series, Rule #2: You Can't Crush on your Sworn Enemy.

Want more Rules of Love Romances? Head on over and grab you next read HERE.
For a full reading order of Anne-Marie's books, you can find them HERE.

Made in the USA
Las Vegas, NV
08 September 2023

77281554R00132